Letters from Home
By: Trina Hawkins

Copyright ©2022 Katrina Hawkins
4-01-2022
All Rights Reserved.

No part of this publication may be replicated, stored, or transmitted, in any format or any means without written authorization. This is a fictitious production from the author's imagination. Names, characters, places, and accidents are part of the imagined world not the real world.

Published by Trina Hawkins
United States of America
Hardcover ISBN: 9798445689348
Paperback ISBN: 9798445662723

Dedication

To my sister, as always, she's there critiquing my work and demanding better descriptions. She's always been pushing me and telling what I need to hear at the right time. Thanks for everything sis!

To my cousins who grew up as close as siblings to me for inspiring me and showing me that life isn't just about living but impacting those around us. You love hard and not afraid to stand up for what you believe. I love you all so much!

To the family that serve the community as nurses and doctors, hopefully I didn't screw it up too much!

To the men and women who sacrifice to protect our nation. Words will never express how much you mean to us, you will never be thanked enough, and you will always be in my prayers. I have friends in different branches of the military, and they continuously inspire me with how much they give and how humble they are.

To my parents for continuing to push me to find my career not just a job. For inspiring me and proving that although some days are terrifyingly hard the good days out-weigh the bad. The list goes on, you know everything you do for me and how appreciated you are.

To my small town of Alert Indiana, and the people I know growing up, you always pull together when someone needs help whether a work day on the farm or sending a card in the mail. If someone hears about a struggle the town pulls together to help their neighbor and shows the true meaning of Christianity. I've learned so much just by watching my elders and can only hope to continue to follow in your footsteps.

To grandma, the strongest lady I know, you set the standard for what we should strive to be like. You have been through a lot and still have an unshakeable faith. I could write a book on just how amazing my family is, and I truly believe that we learned it from you and Grandpa.

My grandpa said he thought I should write about Jesus, to put it in my books. He never saw this book finished but it's dedicated to him. Through all the trials I've faced and asked for advice my grandpa would always give me a hug, smile, and say, "Pray." Sometimes it's hard and I want to throw a fit and scream, but I remember him smiling offering his hand and bowing his balding head. He is missed desperately by family and friends alike but he's singing with the angels and dancing on the streets of gold…probably asking a million questions too.

Warren D. Hawkins Sr.

October 3, 1946- December 12, 2017

Missed but never forgotten.

Contents

Prologue	6
Chapter 1	25
Chapter 2	42
Chapter 3	90
Chapter 4	102
Chapter 5	115
Chapter 6	125
Chapter 7	134
Chapter 8	160
Chapter 9	179
Chapter 10	210
Chapter 11	222
Epilogue	245

Prologue

An old farmhouse set off the road upon a small hill. The driveway curved down across a small creek to the right and back up around to the left up the hill toward the house. The two men slowly drove the car along the drive and parked among the other cars stacked haphazardly at the front of the house. Landon, a Naval Chaplain knew that Thompson was nervous in his marine dress blues uniform. This was the first notification he had to deliver since going through the training. Landon's Naval blue and white dress uniform felt uncomfortably heavy and distracted him from his silent prayer for the upset man sitting beside him. They were silent for a moment, Landon watched Thompson who sighed, delaying wouldn't help them which they both knew. Thompson nodded he was ready, thankful for his companion's silence. Landon got out of the car and started walking up to the old white, two-story house next to him.

The wrap around porch creaked loudly in the darkness around them, Landon took the steps carefully, and glanced at Thompson who seemed fixated on the door. Landon cracked the screen door open and tapped at heavy hardwood front door. Almost instantly a young woman with long dark curls and thin frame opened the door and froze seeing them both. She stepped out and shut the door behind her, Landon heard faint laughter from an inner room as she took in first his stiff uniform and then Thompson's. Landon almost wished they had the wrong house; he could see the shock in her wide eyes and the gleam of tears starting to pool. He knew what she saw: the uniforms and the serious demeanor two men had standing under the porch light. The Navy uniform held the Chaplain badge and insignia on the cuff of his sleeve meaning someone had passed otherwise he wouldn't be there. Landon was surprised she noticed every minute detail.

"May I help you, gentlemen?" she asked, her voice was musical if a little forced. Landon was struggling with the lump in his throat, not sure if he could speak without his voice cutting in and out. Before he could ask her to sit the door flew open and a young girl with a beaming smile and blond straight hair stuck her head out the door. "Skye are you—" she looked at the young lady and then to Landon and Thompson, "Sorry, never mind."

The girl didn't ask any questions but closed the door. Skye looked up at them, her eyes pivoting between Thompson and settled on Landon. He could tell she was trying to keep her shaking voice and emotions tightly controlled, "I'm Skyelar Hamilton…which…I am listed as next of kin to two Marines…my cousin Scout and secondary next of kin to my best friend Johnny. Which one…?"

A tear slipped down, and she dashed it away quickly. Landon's heart sank, he asked God for strength and murmured, "Ms. Hamilton, please have a seat?"

She sat and watched them both stand at attention. Landon had asked Jared just before they started down the long lane toward the house if he needed more time or if he was ready. Now he heard the slow deep breath as Jared prepared himself. Landon prayed she would take it well and not like the last notification where the family blamed the military and cussed the officer out. He prayed that she would be comforted and that he and Thompson had the right words to say, and God would handle the whole situation and guide them.

Thompson held a professional tone as he spoke. Only Landon who had met him and knew him before that night could tell he was emotional and trying to force his voice to stay level and

Letters from Home

professional, "I'm Major Jared Thompson, this is Chaplain Landon King. The Commandant of the Marine Corps has entrusted me to express his deepest regret that John Miles Jr. was killed in action early yesterday afternoon in an ambush. It is classified where he was located at time of death, ma'am. The Commandant extends his deepest sympathy to you in your loss."

Landon stayed silent; Thompson was watching Skyelar. Her face was set, she glanced to Landon, "As his primary next of kin his father was told, correct?"

"Ma'am we have not been in contact with his parents, we have been trying to contact them but the CACO on that team has not found them," Landon paused seeing her swiping her eyes quickly. He had never had a primary next of kin not be found within the timeframe of 24 hours so the coordinator told them to reach Skyelar and inform her. He held in his curiosity to what the story was behind her having two Marines she was next of kin to, as the young lady fought for control to calm herself, fighting the tears as they coursed down her face, and cleared her throat.

"Leave it to Johnny to make it my job to tell them," she half chuckled, and half sobbed, "He tried to put me in charge of everything for him and Scout both, so his parents wouldn't have to see the car pull up. I told him I'd do as much as they'd let me, but he made a will that said I was to take care of everything. Right down to the funeral arrangements."

"Ma'am we still notify them," Thompson glanced to Landon, his training taught him that it was his duty to inform the next of kin and help the primary next of kin if they had any questions about the process. Thompson waited and met her eyes when she straightened on the porch swing. She was handling it well, but Landon wanted to make sure she knew

Letters from Home

she wouldn't have to tell them if she didn't have to, "We will notify them if you like."

"They are on their annual camping trip on their property," she stood up and swiped her eyes again, "Is your vehicle four-wheel drive? If you don't mind, I can show you the way. Mr. Miles likes to go so deep in the woods it would take you a long time to find it since it's dark out. Mr. Miles will want any details you can give anyway."

Landon picked up that she understood the protocols of Notification and that being overseas on a mission they couldn't give all the information to the family because the Marines could still be active in the area or there could be an investigation.

"I am to give you this," Jared murmured and held out the dog tags and the notification letter. She swiped her eyes and Landon noticed Thompson was barely holding it together, aware that this affected him as well, to see her suffer a loss and be the bearer of bad news.

"Let me grab a jacket and flashlights," she turned, and Landon stepped toward her.

"Ma'am, you have guests, if you want to point us in the right direction or we can wait until morning," he offered but she was already shaking her head.

"It's a friend's birthday party and I've known them for years, they can finish the party and lock up when they are done," she shook her head, "I'll be right back. Let me just grab my keys."

Skyelar turned to the door and left it open as she grabbed her keys and glanced into the living room, "I'll be back girls."

Letters from Home   9

Alara and Laikynn sat on the loveseat, pizza sat on the coffee table in front of them. Nadira and Adelina sat cross legged on the floor, Zaidee, Serabeth, and Rashel sat on the couch all watching a movie for Sera's birthday. When she spoke, they all turned, Adelina had told them a Marine was at the door and Skye seemed upset.

"What's going on?" Adelina asked seeing her glassy eyes and flushed face, Skye never cried, and they were worried.

"I can't talk about it, I have to go, feel free to stay for a while," she went out the door and looked at the Chaplain, "Did you say it was four-wheel drive?"

"Yes, ma'am," he walked behind Thompson and Skye as they went to the GMC Yukon. Both men were silent as she sat in the backseat letting them sit in front. The Chaplain drove and Major Thompson informed her that a Casualty Assistance Calls Officer would contact her within 24 hours about death benefits and he would assist her with the funeral arrangements if she needed. He had been aware of the Will that Miles had in place giving her the responsibility otherwise he would have told the father these details. She knew a majority of these officers came from the nearest city so asked, "Are you from Nashville then?"

"Yes, ma'am," the Major nodded looking back at her for some idea why she wasn't asking questions about the information he was giving her.

"Welcome to Elizabethtown, Tennessee," she sighed, "Turn here."

She gave directions going through town and driving highway 40 for about 20 miles over a beautiful mountain and down the other side before she had Chaplain King pull off onto a dirt road. When they stopped at the end of the road there was nothing but forest surrounding them. They both looked around for a moment as the sound of the woods entered the car, the motor off, they could hear the crickets and night sounds. Three other cars were parked there but there wasn't any camp site they could see. Skye steeled herself, "You both ready?"

"Yes, ma'am," they murmured, watching as if expecting her to breakdown or something. Skye had to compartmentalize if she was going to get through this without crying, she could breakdown in private where no one could see. She promised Johnny she wouldn't cry in front of his parents. Skye got out and started hiking through the woods, deftly bypassing creeks and they walked past a cliff. The sight of the valley below the cliff in the moonlight was breathtaking. Skye didn't see the beauty; she was on a mission as she picked her way by her phone's flash light. She heard a gruff voice demand who was there as she approached the clearing the Miles family camped at every year since she was little. She would always recognize John Miles Senior's voice anywhere.

Skye announced herself and the Miles family stood from their various lawn chairs around the fire. Skye had declined to go camping since she had Sera's birthday they had planned. The Miles family always had the camping trip on school breaks, so it floated between weeks.

"Skye?" John Miles frowned confused; Skye rarely had time to visit with her schedule. This late she would have never hiked just to see them, and the two men were still in shadows but he had a feeling something was wrong.

"Sit down I have some news," she watched everyone in the Miles family sit, Johnny's older sister Jayla and her family were camping there as well as Jayden her twin and Jayden's family. Fifteen people sat waiting for Skye to explain what was going on. Skye stepped closer and turned to the two men who stood at attention in shadow behind her.

Letters from Home

"Who is that?" Julie Miles, Johnny's mom asked as John grabbed her hand and closed his eyes. Skye couldn't do it, she wanted to do it but if she tried to talk through the lump in her throat, she'd lose what control she did have.

"Sir," Major Thompson stepped forward, "Are you John Miles Sr.?"

It was a long night, everyone cried, and the Marines offered to drive them back to town since the Miles family were no longer in the mood to sit around a campfire. The Chaplain and Major helped them pack the camp up in the dark, Skye helped fold the tents and packed stuff down to Julie's SUV. When everything was packed up and they got it in the cars the Chaplain drove Julie's car back, Jayla's husband drove them to the Miles house in town since they lived four hours out of town. The Major drove Skye and Jayden's younger boys since the family tossed everything haphazardly into the vehicles in a hurry. They had cried themselves out and were sleeping in the backseat. Skye was exhausted, as soon as she got a signal she called work, "Elizabethtown Hospital."

"I need the on-call doctor, it's Dr. Skyelar Hamilton."

"Hey Skye, one second," the nurse didn't stop to tell her who it was. Skye didn't notice the surprise cross Thompson's face as she looked out at the woods waiting.

"Doctor Guthrie," the male voice murmured in her ear. Doctor Guthrie was her late grandmother's doctor. The hospital was small but as long as someone covered your shift and nothing major was happening you could miss work for emergencies. Skye was worried about the Miles family, she had to wrap her head around Johnny being gone, it really hadn't hit her completely, but she knew in the quiet, alone, it would hit and hit hard.

Letters from Home

"Dr. Guthrie it's Skye. I just got some bad news and need to take a few days off. I will call tomorrow, but I'm supposed to be in at six tomorrow morning and that's not going to happen. All my case notes are up to date, I can go over it with the doctor in the morning if you need me to."

She was relieved it was Guthrie who ran the hospital, he knew she never missed unless something huge happened. She had covered for him two weeks before for a family loss, and he knew how close Scout, Skye, and Johnny were and what that meant to Skye.

"What's wrong, Skye," the fatherly concern she knew so well was evident, "Are you alright?"

He had said that exact same thing when she was a panicking twelve-year-old trying to help her grandma who struggled through chemo and had gotten the flu with a high fever. Her grandpa had fallen the day before and broke his hip and Scout was with him at the hospital. Doctor Guthrie got the answers he needed and made a house visit since the flu was going around bad and could make her grandma worse if she had gone to the hospital. He was a mentor and made her realize that she wanted to be a doctor someday, he helped her make that dream a reality.

"I don't want anyone to know yet until the family is ready to tell people, but I'm listed as next of kin for Johnny Miles, and he passed away. I'm going to be taking care of Julie and John Miles and bringing Johnny home."

"Take all the time you need; I will let Walsh know and we'll cover your shifts. If we have any questions over your case notes we will call."

"Thank you," she hung up before she cried on him. Thompson glanced at her and she noticed he looked wrung out, she knew how doctors had to give bad news and understood what it felt like to give bad news to family members. "Are you alright, Major Thompson? I know giving bad news is rough."

"I'm fine, how are you?" he met her gaze as he drove.

"I'm okay," she sighed, "We are about twenty minutes out still."

Skye yawned and continued to look out at the woods and the moon flashing through the trees. One of the boys in the back was making a puff sound with each exhale that was surprisingly calming. Thompson cleared his throat gently and murmured, "You had mentioned you are next of kin to Scout and John Miles. How are you related or know both of them? If you don't mind me asking."

"Scout is my cousin; Johnny grew up down the road from us and his parents worked so my grandparents babysat all of us. My parents passed in a car accident, Scout's parents were with them as well, so we were raised together by my grandparents, closer than most siblings and was always in trouble."

"So, John Miles was a neighbor your grandparents babysat with you and your cousin."

"Yes," Skye nodded, "We lost so much so young that we practically adopted him and each other as family. Growing up was interesting with those two. You couldn't turn around without a prank being played. They superglued my doll house my great aunt sent to me for my eighth birthday so that I couldn't open it, just because they wanted me to play outside with them."

"Were they always playing pranks?"

"The last phone call I had from Scout he said he had to tell Johnny to quit because it was getting out of hand," Skye smirked, "Scout said they were getting elaborate and feisty, so he had to put a stop to the pranks but Scout in the same breath

Letters from Home

said he missed being able to join in the fun. He is in command and can't so therefore Johnny shouldn't either."

"I bet you have a lot of stories about the pranks they pulled."

"Yeah," she sighed, "I really wish I could call Scout and hear him and know he's okay. They were closer than brothers and I'm worried about him, they are on blackout, and I haven't heard from them in a week. The last conversation I had with Johnny, I told him to make sure Scout remembers to brush his teeth and that I love him. Now I wish it was something a little better than babysit my cousin."

"I'm sure he knew," the Major smiled, "Where are they unloading the camping stuff?"

"Julie won't want to deal with it tonight," Skye shook her head.

They pulled into the Miles house, a little brick one story house. Julie told them to go, "Skye has to work in the morning, you've done enough to get us home."

She turned and walked away. Skye looked at Jayla and flashed an encouraging smile that fell quickly, "I'll take care of the boys. Go hug your mom because it will mean more from you."

Skye and Jayla's husband carried the boys in and laid them on the couch. Skye got the coolers and put the food in the fridge and found John Miles leaning on the counter watching her. "It's late Skye, you have work tomorrow."

"I told them I was taking some time off," she met his lost gaze, "I'm sorry I ruined your vacation, Mr. Miles. I thought you would want the news as fast as I could get it to you."

"Thank you," he spread his arms for a hug, "Johnny loved you so much."

She forced the tears away as she tucked her head under his chin the same way she did every time he hugged her when he found her upset or stressed. Taking care of their grandparents was rough for her and Scout; Johnny helped a lot, but John saw the concern and worry when he'd stop in to pick up Johnny. Toward the end of her grandmother's chemo, he came by with food and Skye had asked why he brought food. He said Johnny refused to leave and Skye shouldn't worry about feeding him with what they had. Julie came and cooked and helped as much as she could after she got off work and all because Johnny refused to leave his friends to deal with the struggle of helping both grandparents by themselves. John was constantly checking in even after her grandmother passed and Johnny practically lived with them after that.

John had joked back then that if her and Johnny ever married, he'd inherit another daughter but Johnny and Skye both knew that would never happen. They thought of each other as siblings, never anything more than friends. "Johnny made me swear to take care of you and Julie for him. He loved you and didn't want you guys to have to deal with everything for him."

"So, the goof decided to make you do it for him," John chuckled, "Such a slacker."

Skye chuckled through the tears and swiped her eyes, "Doctor's orders are to get at least a little sleep. I will take care of the camping gear and be back in the morning."

"Thank you, Skye, but you don't have to," he sighed pushing her hair out of her face.

"I want to," she nodded and felt herself running her hand over the dog tags in her pocket, "I think you should have this."

"Thank you," he slipped the necklace over his head and rubbed the dog tags, "I almost can't believe it."

Letters from Home

"I know," she walked him to the bedroom where Jayla, Jayden, and Julie slept. She went to find the twins' husbands asleep in their old room. She noticed the wall between the bedrooms with all their medals, Johnny had tons of sports medals, but she knew there were four things in his room that he kept and considered more important than the awards. Mrs. Walls' letter, one summer Johnny called Skye and Scout to meet him in town. He had overheard that Mrs. Walls' husband was hurt in a farming accident and he called most the high school to help around their farm. That Saturday Skye had picked and helped Mrs. Walls canning her garden, the boys bailed twenty acres of hay, mucked out the stalls in the barn, and other girls repainted the fence.

A service token from a retired Army veteran sat next to the letter on the shelf above Johnny's bed, Skye didn't open the door but knew exactly what the room looked like. The token was for pushing the man's broken car down to the auto shop. He had been waiting for his mom to finish shopping and had been bored.

A card from a little girl, his senior year a little girl had lost her dog. Johnny had been exercising and he would run to Skye's grandparents' house which was a mile there and back. He found the dog and called the different vets in the area trying to find the owner. The little girl had sent a thank you card to him with a drawing of her and her dog.

The final item was the first pocket knife he ever owned, Scout, Skye, and their grandpa had bought it for him for Christmas the first year he came to town. He used that knife all the time but each year his family or Scout would get him a new one for Christmas, so he retired it to his room to keep. He had other things from his family in his room that were important but those were his favorite things.

Letters from Home

She noticed the Chaplain and Major weren't in the house. She went out and found the SUV and most the trucks unloaded into the garage, stacked neatly. She grabbed a tent and another chair walking it to the garage and once everything was packed in, they shut the garage door, and locked the house up. The Major asked if they wanted him to stay but John said they were alright. They drove Skye home in exhausted silence, the only break was the quiet directions back to Skye's house from the backseat where she sat again. She found Rashel and Adelina there still when she invited them in.

They were cleaning the house from their party; Adelina was sweeping the living room floor and Rashel was doing dishes. When they came to the house both girls stopped to find them all three as if in a daze.

The girls that were at the birthday party for Sera were Skye's friends, they were close and met all the time. Adelina was like an adopted sister since she was still in high school, but Adelina lived with her great-aunt. The group adopted her to give her people closer in age to hang out with, talk to, and keep her out of trouble since she was sent to her great-aunt because she was constantly in trouble at home.

"What happened?" Adelina asked confused.

"We went to get the Miles family," Skye sat exhausted, "Johnny was killed in action. Don't say anything until the family has a chance to, okay?"

"Oh, Skye," Adelina instantly swiped tears and bent to hug her tight, "How are they taking it?"

"None of them are taking it well, they were camping, and we packed them up and took them home before coming back. I'm going over there tomorrow but I just want some alone time."

"If you need anything call me," Rashel nodded and touched Adelina's shoulder, they left quietly.

"Do you want to talk, ma'am?" the Chaplain asked. Skye was amazed again at how they treated the family. Marines were serious about protecting and treating the family like their own flesh and blood. It was one thing to hear about it and another to witness and experience it. Skye knew they were just as exhausted as she was, it took an emotional toll on all of them. The Chaplain was always there for the spiritual aspect but also trained in how to comfort them. The Major was there for any questions. She slowly shook her head. She was tired and just wanted to forget all of it until the morning.

"You can call me Skye, I'm okay, I need some sleep, did you have a hotel room already booked? I have a few guest rooms if you don't and need a place to stay."

"We can get a hotel room, we will see you in the morning," he nodded watching her stand, her shoulders drooped, and she pulled her phone out and called the hotel. The high school had a track meet in town and the small hotel was full.

"I had the rooms made up in case the girls decided to stay. The hotel is full. Please make yourselves at home. The rooms are here," she showed them the two rooms down the hall from the kitchen and didn't notice they watched her walk away slowly, shoulders drooped as she went upstairs. Before sleep took her, she prayed for Scout, Miles family, and for the community effected by the loss. Skye barely heard the phone ring right next to her head near four o'clock and she wondered who would call that early since her shift wouldn't have started until 6AM.

Skye answered, "Hello?"

Letters from Home

Her voice sounded stuffy to her ears, and she heard a sigh and a familiar, exhausted voice murmur, "You were notified I take it?"

"Scout," she forced her voice to not show she was crying, "Are you okay? How is everyone else?"

"Bumps and bruises mostly, haven't really processed it," his voice was quiet as if others were in the room, "Everyone is taking it hard, Skye. We didn't even know they were there until…two others were shot but they were just grazes. I just want to be home, I miss your hugs and your calm, cousin."

"I miss you too," she stood and went downstairs finding the Chaplain there making hot tea at her counter. She sat at the bar and sighed, "It's afternoon there, right?"

The Chaplain looked exhausted but must have heard her phone ring to be awake that early. He motioned to the tea, and she nodded slightly, she focused on the call as Scout hesitated before saying honestly, "I can't sleep," he admitted, "I just keep replaying the whole thing in my head."

"I don't know that I can fix that, Scout," she closed her eyes wishing she could will his bad memories away for him.

"Tell me something, distract me," he sounded desperate, "Skye I need something positive."

"I delivered Victoria's first baby, a little girl," she rubbed her eyes that was one of the most exciting things to happen to her all week, Victoria was a girl from his class who was just married, "Her name is Rosalee."

"I never thought they'd get married," he closed his eyes, "School over yet?"

"Three more weeks and Sera is teaching summer school for the special ed kids," Skye murmured, "Princess Evie is

Letters from Home   20

visiting over the weekend to the farm. Last night was Sera's birthday party which we had a movie and pizza. I have three more babies I will be catching in the next month. Guthrie wants me in the ER more than an OBGYN, so I've agreed to taking more shifts in the ER."

Her friend Serabeth was the Special Ed teacher at school. Scout and Skye had known her for years, her niece was one of the few kids that her friends ever babysat. Sera's mom and Sera raised Evie and when they both worked the group of friends pooled together to watch Evie. Rashel worked on her dad's farm so she watched Evie the most, which was fun considering Evie loved the animals.

She talked softly about everything that had been happening since they had talked last and heard snoring soon after. Scout fell asleep, Skye had to do this before, his responsibility to his team weighed heavily on his shoulders and he took it personally when someone died. Having Johnny gone was even worse for him. She whispered, "I love you, sleep well."

She hung up and looked at the Chaplain who had just finished making the tea and set a cup in front of her. He sat at the bar as well and was surprised Skye looked over to him and whispered, "Could you pray with me for the platoon?"

He prayed with her, and the day started soon after that, she cleaned her house and sat to write a statement to be released. Skye had sat through the training with John before the boys deployed, getting educated on what to do. The only thing was most the community never thought it would be needed, Skye had paid attention, she would never forget that life was short, and you never knew what would happen.

She went to the Miles residence with the two, the Chaplain driving Skye's vehicle, "I don't want the whole community showing up at their house because they see your car."

Skye made a list of everything that needed done, every step of the journey until Johnny made it home. Then called the funeral home to make an appointment. Around 10am she heard her phone ring, she excused herself from the family since she had been helping make a late breakfast for the family with Julie and answered it. She knew it was Scout seeing the blocked number. She stepped onto the front porch and answered seeing the Major watching the kids in the front yard.

The kids were young, and the adults were distraught so he took the kids so the parents had time to mourn and didn't worry about them. Skye was amazed they didn't leave seeing that she had it well in hand, she had asked them but they both just shook their heads, Landon had said, *'It's more than making sure the family is ok and knowing they have all the information. It's about being here to support them and help them take a day to process. We lost a fellow Marine, they lost a son and brother, this is our way of respecting him and helping his family when they are mourning his loss. We would want the same done if we were gone, that a brother at arms took time with our family and helped them.'*

"Hey Scout," she sat in the porch swing and rubbed her temples as she held the phone between her shoulder and ear.

"I need help writing the press release, my mind is blank and I'm his commanding officer," he sounded tired still and she frowned.

"Did you get any sleep?"

"About two hours," he sighed, "I have ten minutes before I have to go to a meeting."

"Write his achievements, be professional but write from the heart, Scout. He loved his platoon, and he is a Marine that other men strive to be."

Letters from Home

"If I write this, can I read it to you?" he asked.

"Yeah," she nodded, "I love you."

"Love you."

At the end of the day they left, the family thanked Skye for helping them so much. She had sent the press release, listened to Scout's press release, and made arrangements. Johnny had passed days before they were told, he had been on a mission so to protect the rest of the platoon, no one was informed until the body was on its way to the states.

Julie and John were going to Dover where Johnny's body would land; once the mortuary released Johnny he would fly into Nashville where the funeral would take place since he was being buried at the military cemetery there. The community took buses to Nashville. Skye went ahead to say her goodbyes before pulling herself together to be strong for the family. It was a closed casket ceremony. Johnny had made Skye promise to make sure they didn't bury the wrong body in his casket. It stuck with her that conversation and Johnny laughing about it. Skye hesitated with her hand on the wood before everyone else arrived. Mr. Miles and Julie were giving her a moment, preparing for the funeral. Skye ran her hand along the cool wood, hesitating again before opening it, half of her wishing she never had to see this day and the other half hoping that Johnny would push the lid open and joke about pranking her good this time.

Skye shook her head, there was no way it was a prank, no matter how much she wished it was. She lifted the lid before she second guessed herself. Pristine uniform, everything perfect to the point of looking asleep. Skye thought he looked peaceful, and her chest tightened seeing him lying so still. Before the tears threatened, she shut the casket lid again and closed her eyes. He didn't have the faint smirk he always wore

Letters from Home

on his face. When Mr. Miles and Julie came in, John asked, "Did…did he look good?"

"You know the picture for the marines?" Skye didn't look back at them, carefully swiping her eyes so they wouldn't see her crying.

"His serious mug?" Julie asked.

"That's what he looks like," Skye nodded. Julie couldn't stand the thought of seeing her baby without a smile on his face and didn't want to see him in the casket. She wanted to remember him alive, and Mr. Miles agreed with her.

The Major and Chaplain were touched by the community, they had seen firsthand how close the community was and were surprised with the way they responded to the loss. It was like a large family that they never expected to see when they first arrived with the news. The Major, at the end of the funeral, touched Skye's shoulder as she slipped into the back office for a drink of water. She turned to find another Marine standing there, he had green eyes and light brown hair, "Major who's your friend?"

"This is Kyle," he murmured quietly, "You were listed to receive everything in Miles' kit."

"Let's take that to my car," she murmured, "I don't think Julie can take much more."

Chapter 1
Pen Pals

Skye sat with her feet underneath her as she listened to the phone call from her cousin Scout. He was an officer in the Marines, deployed overseas in Iraq, and although it was his third deployment, he was homesick. He oversaw a lot of men and constantly worried about them. She listened to him in silence, knowing he had to talk to someone and most the guys there were subordinates to him. She wore a thin t-shirt and night shorts; it was late and blistering hot. It had been just a few short months since the death of their best friend Johnny. Skye half expected a phone call from him and then remembered he wasn't with Scout, she didn't cry or feel broken, but Scout progressively called more often as the months passed.

Skye had to be up at 4am but she knew he needed her. The three were raised together so they were closer than most siblings since their grandfather was the cousins' sole caregiver growing up. Skye went through her second year of college as they deployed overseas the first time, she was up at all hours then too, so he knew he could call anytime, and she was fine with it. Johnny was inseparable from him; they went through basic and everything together. They rarely went more than a day without talking and now Johnny was gone. Scout felt lost without talking to Skye, needing contact with a familiar voice that would understand what he was experiencing.

"They all are homesick not just me, if I didn't talk to you or get your letters, I'd be worse," he admitted, "I love getting your letters….my officers here even get depressed because there is nothing in the mail for them."

"They need pen pals," Skye said softly smiling.

"That's perfect!" he exclaimed, "Can I ask you a favor?"

Letters from Home 25

He always jumped on an idea or comment when it came from her, she stifled a groan, he thought she was smarter than anyone else in the world and could do no wrong. She knew he would ask her to find pen pals for his guys. "You want me to round up some writers?" she yawned softly, "I have a lunch date with Sera and the girls. With the media hitting the military hard nowadays they were talking about needing to show support instead of just throwing money at the charities to help the VA. I can ask them what they think."

"You are the best!"

"I don't know that it will help them with homesickness though," she frowned, "I mean wouldn't that make it worse?"

"You don't get it," he sounded amused that she didn't get something since he claimed she was the smartest person he knew, "It isn't that we want to go home, we just miss hearing about home and having the connection. Tell whoever you can get to write letters and I will get them to those that need it most. Once they have a response, they can send directly to them or you can just send it all to me either way."

"We might just make it a weekly meeting and write while we are together, I can figure it out on this end," she shook her head knowing she was committing to this just because the excitement and energy in his voice at just the thought of his guys getting mail made her want to help.

"You are the best cousin a man could have," he grinned.

"Well, I am glad you know it," she chuckled, "Listen I have to get up in three hours, so I need to get some sleep."

"I forgot it's late over there," he sighed, "Alright Doc Skye get some rest your patients will need you."

"Don't I know it," she smiled, "Love you."

Letters from Home

"Love you more," he chuckled, "Get some sleep."

"Yes, sir," she mock saluted even though he couldn't see her. She was tired but grateful he couldn't see her.

"You totally saluted didn't you," he laughed knowing her well.

She sighed, nothing got past him, he was like the older brother she had wanted but she came to realize it had disadvantages as well. He knew everything even when he was away, and he intimidated all the guys into never asking her out because if they broke her heart, he'd break their face. Skye had overheard such a conversation before. The good memories always outweigh the bad; him refusing to play with the other boys on the playground because Skye was shy and didn't make friends when they both transferred to the school in Elizabethtown. He played with her and introduced his new friends to her, Johnny helped there too when he moved in a few years later. Skye slowly made friends, but Scout and Johnny were her first real friends she made when her parents passed. She remembered Scout would sit with her when she had a nightmare and woke him up, he would talk until she calmed down enough to go back to sleep.

"I'm practicing for when you come home," she chuckled shaking the cobwebs of memories from her vision and heading to her room, "Alright be safe, I love you, and I will let you know tomorrow night if I have writers or not."

"Sounds good, love you too," he hung up heading back to his claustrophobic tin can of an office. He had finished eating and had called her out of needing a listening ear after breakfast. Even though he couldn't tell her exactly what was going on he found comfort in knowing someone back home truly cared about what he was going through. As he started work at his desk, Skye was thousands of miles away going to sleep,

Letters from Home

preparing to get up early and work in a few hours. There was about 7 hours between them, and he wondered if she got tired of the late-night calls or if she missed him just as much as he missed her.

Skye woke up on time and went to work, stopping for a second cup of coffee she felt ready to get the day going. Her hospital was a small one with an emergency wing on the west end of the hospital. They had ICU above it, offices on the east wing with delivery and specialists above them. The main doors led to the nurses station where they directed you right or left to ER or office waiting rooms. It looked like any typical hospital except because they were a small-town people came to the hospital for normal office visits. Skye had been visiting the hospital since her move to Elizabethtown since her grandmother was diagnosed with cancer and went through Chemo. When she finally graduated, she came home to do what she loved. Scout and Johnny were deployed off and on during that time, which made her focus all the harder on her studies.

She had four surgeries and finally 1pm rolled around for her lunch meeting. She worked early so she could get off for a little bit for a much-needed break with friends. She sat with her five friends: Zaidee, Laikynn, Alara, Serabeth, and Nadira. They all became friends at some point or other but like all good friendships they seemed to have known each other for eons.

"Scout asked for a favor," Skye sat down being five minutes late, "Sorry I'm late, surgery ran over."

"I don't want to know what kind," Zaidee interjected before Skye could explain why it ran over.

"What kind of favor," Alara smiled knowing Zaidee would get sick just hearing about the surgery. When they grew up

Letters from Home

together, they used to tell nasty stories just to watch her turn green and get sick almost instantly. She had a vivid imagination and could visualize exactly what they were telling her, she didn't like blood, guts, or anything to do with hospitals, vets, or doctors. It was still amazing to them that Zaidee could be friends with Skye who was a doctor and Laikynn who was a veterinarian.

The restaurant was one of the few in town that they went to that allowed them some away time from work or family. The barn style room had rough walls, old wooden long tables with lamps and deer antler chandeliers, pictures of families that live in the area, some old and faded of people long passed, some new with brilliant colors. Many didn't know that it was a barn back in the day. The wood floor creaked something awful, but the food was amazing, and people came from all over the state to eat Marjorie's from scratch pies and home cooking. Marjorie ran the restaurant like a general in war, barking orders and making sure everyone had sweet tea. Her husband was a veteran, and she honored the small town's veterans retired or abroad with pictures on one wall. The girls always sat at the military wall, it had old and new pictures, but a corner was set for the Marines, all of them unsmiling in uniform. The small community always supported each other and a majority of the population at Elizabethtown was military or military families. So having the military wall was tradition and reminded everyone to pray for the military and their leadership. At least that was the sign at the front of the building.

Skye found it difficult to come to the Diner the past few months because of one picture. Marjorie always put a black filmy material over those that were deceased recently, if they had passed over a year, she would move the pictures to a wall dedicated to those they all had lost. Skye avoided looking at the walls, no matter if she wanted to see Scout's unsmiling face, she knew one Marine right next to his picture, also unsmiling but so close to her heart, was wrapped in the black see-through material and she didn't want to cry.

When Johnny passed it was like her heart shattered into a million pieces. She forced herself to focus and to keep the tears from coming, it took her a while to do it as she looked at the old, laminated menu studying the old paper with barn wood printed in the background, barbed wire around the edges, the Times New Roman font with the Spur bullet points of each meal option. Once she calmed down, she started explaining what Scout needed.

Skye talked fast for a while, they agreed that it was fine if it meant seeing each other as well. Being in different fields meant they had to strategically plan to get everyone together in the same room. They were excited to try something new and get to see each other more often. It was a good idea although Sera brought up a good point, writing was one thing, but she wanted to make sure these marines wouldn't think anything more of them than pen pals. Skye had agreed she would tell Scout their concerns and offered to have a weekly meeting at her house; they agreed to go there at the end of the week to finish their letters. Skye went back to do her stint of emergency rooms and between a fractured arm in one room and kidney stones in the other she called Scout.

"Get sleep last night?" he greeted her heading toward chow for supper.

"Not much but I'm surviving on cold coffee," she looked at the x-ray of the arm, "I'm doing ER, so this will be quick. I have five writers and I will write too, that makes six. Is that enough for now?"

"Yes, when do you plan to send them?" he glanced at one of his officers waiting for him to end the call. They had an in brief in ten and before that they needed to go over the information one more time before telling the men what their objective and mission would be for the next outing.

"This weekend, I will put them in the mail on Saturday. You should get them soon from there, right?"

"Yeah," he nodded, "Thanks."

"Got to go, call anytime, love you."

Skye hung up and went back to work; Scout looked to his squad leaders and asked how their men were and if everyone was getting letters from home. Most were, there were quite a few that weren't, and Scout frowned suddenly worried Skye didn't have enough help, "Any of them badly homesick?"

"Oh yes," one nodded understanding this was a concern of Scout's before getting into the paperwork for the in brief, "Before we got here, he was the life of the party, encouraging everyone, now that we've been here for months, he's lost his smile. I don't think I've seen him get one letter yet."

"Who is it?" Scout knew this was many of them but hoped Skye's comment of pen pals would do the trick and get them out of their funk.

"Gryffin Scott."

"I have one like that too, he wasn't the life of the party, but this deployment has been hard on him, he's a scout sniper, Mercer."

"I have two that I can think of at the moment, Wolf and Murphy."

"Quinn and Hayes," the first murmured remembering some more.

"Alright," Scout nodded, "Let's get to business."

Letters from Home

"Why are you asking about that?" his friend James asked as one of the squad leaders—Kane—was called out of the room. Scout knew Kane had a rough time lately and needed a pen pal too, but he didn't want Kane to know it was from him.

"My cousin likes to write letters to me and had mentioned commercials on TV asking for support of the troops. She hates that people just throw money at a problem and thinks they should be more involved. Her friends had agreed a few days ago that people at home need to be supportive of the troops. It got me thinking and I asked her to round up some friends to fix a problem. I think it will be good to have a pen pal, it gives them something to look forward to here and keeps her and her friends busy and out of trouble while I'm away."

"How old is your cousin?" one of the squad leaders asked confused. Scout didn't talk about his family at all, it was business a majority of the time with him. He was a great leader but kept everyone at a distance. They knew that he had his reasons and trusted him enough to not question why.

"26 years old," Scout watched him, "Yes, I still keep tabs on her. No one is to tell them that the pen pals are my idea or that it's anything to do with me. Understood? Not even Kane is to know since he isn't here."

All the leaders understood that it wouldn't be received well if the commander was involved. He would want them to have honest opinions of if this worked or if it actually helped the men without the men knowing their leader was involved. Kane not being there just meant he would give an honest review of the project if he didn't know where the rest would sensor their opinions.

They agreed it was a promising idea and could help their men. Scout sat back and thought about what Kane had said, Mercer was a friend and Scout had noticed a change in him. A few

Letters from Home

months ago, Mercer had been happy and enjoying life. Until a mission went sideways, and he couldn't save his best friend, they had been thick as thieves and usually kept the entire platoon entertained with elaborate pranks or just being in the area. Mercer was the calmer of the two but was the life of the Platoon, he was the guy everyone wanted to have around, he could joke to ease the tension in a room, or he could tell the boldest lie to set everyone to laughing at the mess hall. Naturally it led to the two getting disciplined often, but it didn't stop them. When Johnny Miles was killed in action three months ago and everyone in the community and the platoon were taking it hard. He was a solid guy with a heart of gold.

Mercer and Miles would play with the local kids throwing a ball around or playing soccer, their nickname was M & M. Mercer always made people feel better and encouraged them. Scout felt bad that he had noticed Mercer's change and hadn't done anything about it, knowing it was because his best friend was gone. It wasn't Mercer's fault, the team leader had split them up, Miles went west, and Mercer was east, so Mercer went to high ground and the squad took fire. Mercer heard that Miles was hit by an enemy sniper which Mercer took out, but it didn't save his friend. Mercer blamed himself and Scout knew that was hard to deal with having lost a friend himself that day. Kane entered again and they went over their brief.

When the brief ended, Scout called Skye hoping it was still early enough she wasn't in bed, it was late his time, but he knew she was tired from her early call that morning.

"Three times in one day, I should feel honored but I'm too tired," she answered the phone drowsily.

"Did I wake you up?"

"I just laid down it's 6 here so I technically should still be up, but I am tired. What's up?"

"I have seven people," Scout told her, thinking of Kane as well.

"I can ask Rashel," she thought about it. Rashel was trying to get a field planted since it hadn't rained that morning. She had been rained out of the fields for almost two straight weeks, so she was trying to catch up.

"Thanks, cousin," he murmured, "Get some rest."

"Night, you get some rest too it's late there."

"True," he sighed, "Love you."

Skye called Rashel before she forgot and asked her to be a pen pal for her cousin's platoon. Rashel agreed to write and told Skye she would be there Friday to deliver the letter and talk then. As the week went by all the girls stared at a blank piece of paper trying to figure out what to write someone they have never met. It was anonymous until Scout gave the letters to the men, which made it that much harder. Skye had sent a text saying:

> Be positive nothing negative or downers. They need a few laughs and something to brighten their days.

Skye listened to all her friends sitting around the living room talking about how hard it is to write to someone they have never met. What if they said something wrong? What if they took it the wrong way and wanted a relationship? That wasn't what they signed up for and they didn't want to be the ones to make it worse if they said something wrong. She had told them to pray about it as well to know what to write, they still stressed about writing to complete strangers.

Skye decided to fix the situation, "What if we read them aloud so we can all hear and decide if it's good? We can have Scout read them too just to be on the safe side."

Each girl had tried to write the letter and trashed it several times and most finally just gave up trying for semi-professional and going with how they would talk to someone. They don't know these people and writing to a stranger had them stressed until late the night before. The only one that was half calm was Skye and that was because she wrote letters to a lot of people for any reason. She had written letters since she was around 10 to different people, had been pen pals with several others, and still wrote to a few Marines she remembered being with Scout when he deployed. She tried to keep track of them and send them encouragement occasionally, even though life was sometimes busy.

Alara had read her letter and wrote about a failed do-it-yourself chair she had tried to build. It fell apart and Skye had to ask the obvious question.

"When did you try the chair?" Skye asked confused.

"It happened today," Alara raised an eyebrow, "Don't judge."

Serabeth snorted and everyone laughed hysterically, Alara wasn't one for making things, everything she tried fell apart because she got in a hurry to make it and forgot steps. They all fell silent for a moment. Nadira and Rashel were running late so they started talking about what they could send. Care packages once they got to know the guys, postcards, pictures, and Skye leaned forward as Rashel and Nadira came in.

"Alright who is good with video editing?" she watched them. Scout brought up another blackout may happen, and she knew letters were a little behind during that time so maybe something they could do was a video to send to them, it was

Letters from Home

something she had been thinking about for a while and wasn't sure if it was possible.

"The only one I know of is Adelina," Rashel frowned, "Why?"

Adelina was taking a summer class and had a project. She didn't want to write letters but anything technological she was all about. Skye nearly jumped up and down, if anyone could make a killer video it was Adelina.

"They have blackouts where no communication can be received by the guys. When that happens, I want to have videos for the whole platoon, showing them a flash of our normal day. Have letters on standby for them to open even though it is a blackout that Scout can keep ahold of. Sound good?"

"I'm texting Adelina to see if she can start on that," Rashel nodded, "I think that would be awesome!"

"Oh…kay but I'm not sure how that will work with working in a hospital," Nadira murmured being a front desk nurse at the hospital she was aware of all the HIPPA laws and violating them would be catastrophic.

"We can ask permission or have her cut them out," Skye murmured.

"Sounds good," they agreed.

"Adelina agreed," Rashel smiled surprised at how fast she responded. Adelina was 18 and wanted to go to college for communications, she was always seen around town with a video camera making small movies for her portfolio. She was waiting two years to go to college to save money and make sure she wanted to do just that. She lived down the road from Sera and hung out with them to keep out of trouble.

Adelina agreeing sent them talking fast to think about what else they could do. They left late that night with an idea of what to expect over the next few days. Adelina would be dropping in on them with little to no notice except at the hospital. Skye went to bed, planning to drop the letters in the mail the next day. She hadn't read her letter because honestly, she hadn't finished writing it. She would do that first thing in the morning before she ran to the post office.

She called Scout to let him know the letters were on the way. He said he looked forward to getting them and asked how the girls liked it.

"It'd be easier if they had names and knew them but it's going to be fine," Skye murmured.

Skye knew it took around ten days to get a letter to Scout it also might be more since she used a bigger envelope for all their letters. The girls were excited and already started writing stories down to share with the guys just waiting on a response. She had told them to write a few letters in advance since they were going to have a blackout. She had talked to Scout just before their meeting and he told her they were going to have a blackout in a few weeks. She had Rashel get ahold of Adelina to let her know.

When the house was quiet, she pulled a box out from beside her rocking chair. It held letters tied with ribbon and creased letters she received when Johnny passed away. They had been in his belongings and because he was practically raised with her most his belongings were sent to her to go through for his family. He had told Scout to send all of it to her, so she could make sure everything was in order. It had been hard; she had called off work for three days to go through everything. She had found her letters in his kit folded neatly in a pocket. She had given his family the rest of his things and told his mom about the letters she had written to him that she kept. His mom

Letters from Home

went to his room and handed her a shoe box she had found from his apartment. Skye opened it to find her letters from the first two deployments, and now she read the letters back and forth from the second deployment.

Hey Skye,

This second deployment is different. Scout is learning his new position and they are talking about making him a platoon commander if we go for a 3rd deployment. We were reminiscing about the past. Our guys think it's hilarious hearing about these stories. Scout reminded me of one summer that was one to remember.
Do you remember cleaning out the attic with your grandpa? That was a fun summer! In the attic we listened to grandpa tell stories about each thing we found interesting. Even the letters Scout and I found in an old box. He said they were letters from an angel while he was in the Marines. Scout asked how an angel sent letters and grandpa laughed, "They are from your grandma while I was deployed. She wrote me every chance she got."
I looked at the letters, we were about 10, Scout was 12; I glanced at you, who was looking in other boxes not hearing about the letters. "Skye would write letters to us when we go to the Marines, wouldn't she, Scout?"
"She would for me but why would she write to you," Scout shook his head knowing we were close.
"Because one day I'm going to marry her," I declared, and you surprised us when you walked up soon after that and asked what the letters were. After being told you remember us practically making you swear to write to us when we left for the Marines.
We never once thought we wouldn't go to the Marines, we always just knew. I always thought I'd go to the Marines and be married to you but when you grow up things changed. I still think you need to meet my buddy, Derek. He's quiet but an

Letters from Home

amazing guy. Next time I come home I will see if I can't get him to visit. I probably will stay a bachelor the rest of my life, but you deserve the best, don't forget that. I'm just glad we never married because your cousin may become my commander and how awkward would that have been?

Talk soon,

Johnny

She smiled as she read the letter and then pulled her letter, she wrote back to him. It was funny how when she read this, she wondered why he thought he'd stay a bachelor, but he had been right, he was a bachelor his whole life.

Johnny,

Do you remember growing up playing power rangers, cowboys and Indians, and baseball? Scout made no exceptions because I was a girl. You played with us and a few other boys in town (when we were playing baseball). We mainly played around the farm.
When we went to junior high school for 7th grade year, I noticed both of you in the Marines booth at the job fair in the gym one day. I watched from a distance, realizing one day soon you both would be off saving the world without me. I couldn't even contemplate becoming a Marine, Scout, and grandpa both had tried to teach me about guns, but I didn't like them and didn't want anything to do with them.
I walked around considering what my options were; I had helped grandpa with grandma when she was sick until she passed. I had been young, and grandpa had tried to keep me from being responsible for all the medicine and helping her, but I liked helping grandma, making her feel better.
I went to a booth for RN, CNAs, and started asking a bunch of questions. The nurse was very informative, but it wasn't what I was looking for, the nurse only did so much, I noticed a

Letters from Home 39

guidance counselor standing nearby and went over.
"I want to be a doctor, is there a booth for that?" I demanded seeing Scout and you both still at the booth together getting information on what the steps would be to get to the Marines.
"Are you sure? That's a long road to follow, Skye," the lady didn't understand I had all the time in the world suddenly—I needed something to distract me when my best friend and cousin left me.
"Johnny and Scout are going to leave me to join the Marines, I want to do my part in serving my country and that's by being a doctor," I glared at the guidance counselor.
I was led to an empty booth where a tall man sat looking bored. It was grandma's doctor before she passed. He smiled seeing me, "Hello Skye."
"Dr. Walsh," I rushed my words like I was running out of time already, "I want more information about how to become a doctor, what I need to take here at school, the steps from high school to getting a job at the hospital, and anything else."
After a long talk with Dr. Walsh, I turned to head home and found both of you staring at me like I had lost my mind. I was confused, "What?"
"Why a doctor?" Do you remember asking me that?
"Didn't you get enough of an idea from helping grandma?" Scout asked me.
"You know me the best, Johnny, what would you suggest I do when I graduate high school? What do you see me doing?" Scout wisely kept his mouth shut. We had more of a sibling rivalry and Scout tried to keep it from blowing out of proportion. But I wasn't pushing your buttons, I wanted any idea what you and Scout thought. Going to be a doctor made sense but you two knew me best, so I wanted to see what your ideas were going to be. This time you thought about it and told me that I might be right about becoming a doctor, that I did good helping grandma and keeping track of the pills and what seemed to work best. Dr. Walsh constantly praised me, you

Letters from Home

reminded me, for doing so great a job and he meant it not just encouraging a young lady trying to help her grandma but seeing potential.

"Scout?" you turned to him for some help, usually he stayed out of our conversations that led to arguments but we finally agreed on something.

"I think it's going to take all the smarts you got to go through that much schooling," Scout shrugged, "When you go through college and everything it will be almost 8 years."

"Less if I can take more classes while I'm in high school." You both thought I was crazy to do homeschooling to get the classes I needed because the school didn't offer them. You were mad I graduated three years later (ahead of you and Scout both) and went to the community college for my Gen Eds. When you finally graduated, you both went straight to boot camp. I was in college in the city, so I wasn't so bad when you all left for the first deployment. It took me a while to get used to writing letters. Now I'm a professional letter writer. As far as meeting your friend...Derek?...........I don't think so. I know you, if you like him, I am pretty sure it would be a terrible idea!

Love ya Johnny!

Skye

Chapter 2
First Letters

Scout sat at his desk reading reports and trying to get reports written for his CO when mail was delivered to them. Scout received his groups' mail first. He always checked the mail and put it in order to make it easier on his leaders that took turns reading the names off. He found his own mail and noticed it was thick. He opened the larger envelope to find individual letters folded nicely. He grabbed some envelopes and read the top one.

Scout remembered Rashel from Skye's graduation. She was dark haired and what he considered to be a quiet little farm girl who lived with her dad. He thought Wolf would match well, not that he was a farmer, but he liked being outdoors and their personalities seemed to match. If he was being honest with himself, it would be that he was just flying by the seat of his pants and had no idea how it would work. He didn't have faith like Skye did, he just hoped he guessed right.

The next one was from Nadira. Scout tried to remember her but couldn't place her among all Skye's friends. He hadn't been home in a while so assumed it was a newer friend. He read her letter quickly enough.

Scout had a scrap of paper where he wrote Nadira and Kane and smiled. Kane was levelheaded and liked pranks that were innocent fun like what she described in her letter. Kane was called Dad by most the boys with them since he had kids and got his dad voice on when pranks got out of hand. Scout let him, and the other squad leaders take care of the pranks until someone went too far. He knew they needed to have some fun in the high stress environment and Kane usually caught it before it got too far. He wrote Wolf and Rashel together and read the others. Murphy with Serabeth; Alara with Gryffin;

Quinn with Zaidee; Hayes with Laikynn; and he read Skye's letter to her pen pal:

Hello,

I write letters all the time but always to someone I know. My cousin says this is good for some of you to get a letter occasionally, to keep a piece of home. I write him all the time and know lately it's been rough for you guys. I've been asked to keep it a secret who I am related to, so he doesn't show he worries about his buddies or has a heart (I know better!). As you can probably tell I'm not used to writing to someone I don't know. I guess I should probably start with my name now that I've wasted half the page. I've thrown away at least ten pages trying to start it, so I've promised myself to just write what I'd say...hence the babbling!

My name is Skyelar Hamilton, I am a military brat raised by my grandfather along with my cousin and best friend. I grew up here in this tiny town in Tennessee; I went to college when my boys (cousin and best friend) went to the Marines. I recently graduated with my doctorate, so I am trying to get used to the MD at the end of my name now. I work at the little hospital in our town doing anything from surgeries to regular office visits. Now is summer time so I get a lot of kids coming in for their school shots which are if-y on a good day since half this town is afraid of needles. Maybe later I will tell you my secret to getting shots done when I have an upset little kindergartener in here!

Now, I'm in an old Victorian style white farm house on the edge of town, sitting in my favorite chair writing letters to you and a few other Marines I know in your platoon. I try to write all of them once in a while when I get time, but I swore to my cousin I would never quit writing to him while he's deployed. I made the promise when I was 10 years old in front of my grandpa who was a Marine as well. My cousin and best friend

Letters from Home

made me swear to write to them. Funny how they both knew they were going to be Marines, they had said 'When we become Marines, we need you to write to us. Swear Skye that you will write!' They were both bigger than me and I wasn't going to argue with both of them, so I swore and have kept the promise. What started it all was helping grandpa in the attic. We had run across letters my grandma wrote him while he was deployed. He called them letters from an angel. He confessed grandma wrote them and they helped him remember why he was overseas and gave him a bit of home to keep with him.

I know my old farm house isn't your home, but America is and most of the states have farms, woods, crickets, and deer. Lord knows we have deer a plenty! Unless you live in the desert and then I'd have to insist on moving or at least visiting. The weather here has been cool like the seasons are still trying to change even though it's June. What's the weather like there?

I know you all don't get a lot of free time, so I hope this finds you well and rested. You can write back but it's not mandatory. If you need anything let me know. I am praying for you guys.

Skye

P.S. I was reading Psalms 25 and have been thinking of you guys a lot at least these three versus. It says:

In you, Lord my God, I put my trust. I trust in you; do not let me be put to shame, nor let my enemies triumph over me. (1-2)

My eyes are ever on the Lord, for only He will release my feet from the snare. (15)

I hope these don't offend you, this is what my prayer has been for your platoon lately and I pray for safety and for *endurance, rest, and peace. Semper Fidelis and God bless you.*

Scout stared in surprise; Skye never put scripture in his letters mainly because he told her he didn't know that a god could be loving with so much evil in the world. She didn't push the subject she had just wrote back that without evil no one could love or need God and it proved there was a God, and he gave us a choice to follow him. Scout didn't know she read the bible a lot but the scriptures on the paper in his hand made him feel a little better. To know Skye was praying for them made him feel more peaceful. He wondered what Mercer would say but he didn't care, someone had to get through to him.

Scout finished putting them in envelopes and called James, a squad leader in to pass the mail out. Scout stepped into the bunkhouse. They had been there for almost five months, every day they had different missions and very few days of relaxation. He had an announcement after they finished getting letters. He saw surprise on the seven men's faces. Mercer frowned confused seeing the envelope especially with no return mail.

"Sir?" Mercer stood, "This has no return address and doesn't have the correct information on the envelope."

James glanced at it and frowned seeing he was right it just had Mercer scrawled across it. Scout stepped into the light, and everyone jumped to their feet quickly coming to attention.

"As you were," he murmured and hesitated as they all went back to sitting or lounging, "A few of you will see some letters with just your names on the front. I gave permission for this to happen. Please see me for return addresses and any further questions. I have another announcement for you. We will be going to blackout next month. Our orders are to transfer to

Letters from Home

FOB Camp Leatherneck. Make the appropriate calls home to let them know."

He left hearing murmurs; it was another camp that had seen a lot of war. They were supposed to be there for the rest of their deployment but that didn't mean much since their orders continued to change. They went where they were needed; the Marine saying: first to the fight, was true. The platoons and squads rotated around. By the end of their tour, they were exhausted and ready for home and about the time they got used to being home it seemed they were deployed again.

Alara sat with a small stack of blank loose sheets of paper on the kitchen table in front of her. She had coffee beside the stack and her favorite Tinker Bell pen she used at the hospital. She had thought about her letter a million times and started it at least twice. It was Thursday morning and she had one more day before she had to give it to Skye to send in the mail.

"I can't just write hey, I'm Alara…write me back to make this easier," she mumbled taking a sip of coffee and struggled not to drop it when it burnt her tongue. She stood and got a glass of ice water before sitting again. She had woken an hour early just to have more time to write. "I'm not going to write about burning my tongue either."

She sat the water down and closed her eyes with a heavy sigh. She looked at the gray walls of her kitchen, the sliding glass door behind her brought in the morning sunlight. It was looking like a start to a beautiful day. She glanced outside and frowned, she had to finish her do it yourself project sitting on the porch. Alara had been working hard to make a chair for her porch. It was half done from the pictures and instructions on Pinterest. She would do that later or Friday morning when

Letters from Home

she woke up. She turned around and started to focus, it was hard not having a name for this letter, it made it hard to know what they would think about her life. She sighed and muttered, "I'm not throwing this out no matter how bad it sounds this time! God, please give me the words to say to help whoever gets this letter, Amen."

She grabbed the coffee and looked at the steam, decided water might be safer, she would hate to have to send a coffee-stained paper to her new pen pal. She finally started writing a few seconds later as the light brightened behind her until her cell phone beeped a set alarm for work. She set the water in the sink and drank the hot coffee like it was nothing.

After work she went out to work on her chair. She frowned over the instructions but continued following them. She went to bed at dark and first thing in the morning she continued to work again. She looked at the chair and smiled, it looked right, she snapped a photo for evidence because all the girls knew she wasn't great at following instructions and half the time things fell apart on her. She had painted it a pretty green and it was the perfect height to see the eagle's nest in the tree across the yard. She went to sit, but continued all the way to the ground, it caved in. She heard the dog scramble as if she had tried to shoot it, sliding around to the steps and under the porch. Alara groaned and grumbled, "I need a hobby that I can actually do successfully!"

She groaned getting up and again as she went in, deciding she would ask her pen pal what his were. She felt good about her letter; it wasn't too terrible, so she took it with her to work. After they finished the day, they went to Skye's house.

When the envelopes were passed around by James, a squad leader in the platoon Gryffin was napping in the corner and when his name was called his eyes shot open just as James dropped the envelope on his chest. He caught it before it slid off, sitting up at the same time. There were cots, tables, and laptops around the room. Most the squads all hung out together, he had been watching TV but fell asleep, and now he frowned at the envelope seeing just his first name on the front.

It wasn't allowed for them to get mail without it having the correct information and he glanced up finding Mercer standing saying the same thing. Looking around he noticed a few others in the room holding envelopes curiously. He jerked to his feet when Platoon Commander Chase stepped into the room. He sat back as soon as he said, "As you were."

Scout Chase explained some of what was going on and he opened the letter curiously.

Hello,

This is hard because I don't know you and when I go to write it's like blank slate, nothing. It's not that I don't want to write but that I have a tough time writing to someone I've never met. So hopefully you can clear that up soon.
I guess I should start with my name, Alara Martin. I have a younger brother who is in the Marines. Last time I talked to him was last week and he was heading into scout sniper training. I am a nurse; I work with Skye who started this pen pal mission as she calls it. I'd call it Letters from Home although technically this town isn't home to you it's America and that's home enough. We are planning to write often. I have never had a pen pal so I'm not exactly sure what to write or if we will have much in common but it's worth a try at least. What are some of your hobbies? I'm looking for something new to try, last project I tried went sideways, literally, I tried to build a chair, it collapsed as I sat in it so maybe something

Letters from Home 48

easy to start with (no power tools because that's a downfall). So, I hope this got you to laugh, at least that would make the bruise worth it. I mean my dog acted as though the world was ending and tail tucked scampered off the porch and under it to hide. So, I'm going to steer clear of DIY projects for a while. Hope everyone gets well deserved sleep and our thoughts and prayers are with you all.

Sincerely,

Alara.

Gryffin laughed; how could a girl mess up a chair? She definitely asked the wrong guy for hobby ideas. He was an adrenaline junky. They called him Gryffin instead of Scott because they joked that as much as he was jumping out of planes and in the air, he should be a griffin with big wings.

"What's so funny, Gryffin?" one of his squad buddies asked.

"This letter!" he grinned.

"Read it out loud," another demanded, and he read it out loud, they all burst out laughing, joking that she asked the wrong guy. When they all calmed down, he decided he wanted to write this nurse back, looking around he found Kane. He came into the room with extra paper and pens. He stood and followed Kane to a table. The guys that got the letters all sat together. Gryffin glanced around finding Wolf, Murphy, Quinn, Hayes, and Kane with him.

"I thought Mercer got a letter," he murmured glancing at Mercer who was in his usual place in the corner tossing a stress ball up in the air with one hand his other behind his head laying on his back.

"He did," Kane murmured, "Maybe he will in private."

"He's had it rough the last few months," Hayes murmured, "He needs a good distraction."

Gryffin agreed but didn't say anything as he focused on the paper and realized how Alara must have felt staring at the paper. It was hard to write to someone you knew so little about. He glanced at Murphy to find his eyes on him.

"What?" Gryffin asked confused.

"Dude I'm thinking," Murphy frowned, "This is hard."

"Just think they didn't have any idea about us and they wrote us. Just pretend you are talking to this girl on messenger or something," Kane frowned at them.

Gryffin decided he needed a quiet place to think and stood, "I need quiet to write anything."

"Don't forget to get with Chase to get her address," Wolf murmured as he walked away.

Gryffin decided to write the letter before getting the address. He wrote and put it in the envelope before going to Chase's office. It was early in the morning, and he heard murmuring before he tapped at the door.

Scout Chase called to enter as he ended the phone call and watched Gryffin step in, "Sir I came to ask for the address for Alara?"

"Of course, come take a seat," Scout murmured.

Gryffin sat and pulled a small notepad out of his breast pocket and wrote her address. Scout waited as he wrote it neatly and then asked how Gryffin liked the letter. "She seems to be funny. I need a good laugh, sir."

"Good to hear," Scout murmured.

Letters from Home

Gryffin thought over his letter and smirked, "I gave her a few hobby ideas. I kinda feel sorry for her asking for hobbies from me. I mean I base jump, and the safest thing I do is hike and camp."

Scout smirked, "She asked you. If she needs something safer, she can ask her friends."

Gryffin set the letter in the mail and wondered when the next letter would be coming, he didn't get a lot from home and he missed it, he missed hearing women speaking their minds and wearing what they wanted. The culture here was so different than home he missed it the most. All he could do was wait for the next one to come.

Hello Alara,

My name is Gryffin Scott. I couldn't imagine being a nurse, I don't have great bedside manners, I'm the guy that yells to put some dirt on it and keep going…I think that's just the Marine way though.

I seriously died laughing when I read your letter. I think the whole platoon read your letter because I couldn't stop laughing. How do you build a chair and it fall apart? I'm still chuckling, I'm not laughing at you, obviously you are smart to be a nurse, but you might be right in avoiding power tools for a while!

Some hobbies of mine, now I have the blank slate! Hm…I like to sky dive, base jump, I'm an adrenaline junky so rock climbing and if you can't tell I like heights. Some easy stuff though is fishing and hunting. I live close to the Rocky Mountains, so I like to hike and am outdoorsy. I'm not sure if we will have much in common but you could probably write anything, and I'd be glad for the letter. It's the thought that counts and we appreciate the prayers and letters.

Letters from Home

If you decide to try any of my hobbies, be sure to let me know how it goes, make sure you take someone with you if you do rock climb and someone that's experienced, I don't want my pen pal getting hurt because she tried something dangerous, nurse or not.

Keep the prayers and letters coming, we are getting ready to have a blackout so please number your letters. It's next month and if you don't get a letter back that's probably the reason. We don't get a lot of time to write so some letters may be super short. Speaking of that, it's time for chow so I got to go!

Write soon, thanks again!

Gryffin.

Serabeth raced around the house trying to find her keys, her mom was dressing her niece, Genevieve. Serabeth called her Evie or her little princess, she had custody of Genevieve since her brother was lost to the war. Serabeth tried to stay positive, Shawn (her brother) was always positive so she tried to be the same for Evie's sake.

"Mom I can't find my keys!" she complained.

"I haven't seen them, sweetie," her mom, Gwen frowned, "Evie what is in your pocket?"

There was silence, Serabeth continued to look, it was summer school, so she had ten minutes to get out the door and down to the other side of town to the school. She had slipped on flip flops, not caring what the school policy was since she was running late. Her mom laughed, "Princess Evie has your keys in her pocket, she doesn't want Aunt Sera to go."

"Evie!" Serabeth shook her head, "Don't scare me like that, I thought I lost them!"

Evie handed them over with a pout as Sera kissed her forehead and ran for the door, "Bye love you!"

She raced to the school, she was a special needs teacher and worked as a tutor over summer, mostly with the special needs since they always fell behind. At least the school didn't just pass them like most the schools she had shadowed at during college. She loved her school, she parked in someone else's parking spot and raced inside finding the principal there frowning, "Evie tried to hide my keys!"

"Little princess is getting smart!" he chuckled, "Keep real shoes in your car for next time, Serabeth!"

"I will," she laughed as she went to the class and called order. She went through class, during her prep and lunch she wrote, she didn't have much trouble, trying for semi-funny but not too much. She went home that night to find a note saying to meet her mom and Evie for supper in town that they were getting their toes done at the nail salon while they waited for school to end.

Serabeth went to the nail salon and found them sitting side by side at the end, there was a mini throne for the little girls that came in to sit as the princess of the hour. Evie called her grandma Gigi and Serabeth was Belle—as in Beauty and the Beast because she worked at a school with a *huge* library.

After supper and late that night Serabeth finished her letter and prepped for the next day. Gwen had to work in the morning, so Rashel was going to watch her and show her around the farm. Serabeth put two extra sets of clothes, socks, underwear in the backpack and set the backpack by the refrigerator to remember the lunch box filled with tons of snacks and lunch.

Letters from Home

Brian Murphy was playing Euchre with some of his friends in the rec room. When mail was delivered, as was custom the squad leader would pass it out, if you didn't move fast enough, they would toss it to you, and more accurately miss you completely. At least that was how James worked, fast as possible, Brian noticed Gryffin had caught his to his chest as he sat up in surprise. Mercer was in the corner and surprisingly James set it in his hand when he tossed his stress ball into the air, Brian was pretty sure it wasn't a stress ball but a Nerf ball that he and Miles would toss back and forth and play with the local kids with. Now he tossed it straight up in the air and caught it as he laid on a cot in a quiet corner of the room.

When Brian glanced up, hearing his name called, he found an envelope flying directly at his head and caught it just in time. James was on to the next person and didn't notice but Wolf laughed and told him nice catch. He wondered who could have sent the letter but noticed about the time Mercer stood up that it didn't have a return address and only had Murphy across the envelope. It wasn't allowed to happen like that, all mail was designated to an individual correctly or it was withheld.

Once Chase explained and left Brian sat down and studied the envelope for a moment. He opened it curious to see what it was about and found a neatly written letter, it was from a girl by the writing, he didn't even have to read it. Her letters were half cursive and half printed but it made it look interesting on the page. He read it quickly.

Hello,

My name is Serabeth, I was asked to write by a friend. We decided we were going to support our men/women overseas by

Letters from Home

writing—believe me I miss spell check and my handwriting is rough at best so bear with me. I'm not the best speller in the world and my grammar is terrible!

I have a younger brother who just started his first year of college, he is going for engineering, and I know he can do it because he's super smart. I told him he could build me a house when he finishes but he laughs like it's a joke. I don't find it funny; I want a log cabin with some acreage, but he says he's not looking to build houses he wants to build engines and bridges. I told him we would talk when he passed his first semester of English. He isn't laughing anymore; he calls me to proofread his papers it's hilarious his teacher is a grammar Nazi! I don't tell him I send it to Nadira to proofread, she's another friend and pen pal to you guys. ☺

I am a special needs teacher at the local school. I teach everything but I'm best at math and science. My students are unique and easily loveable. I teach 6th-8th grade, but with them being special needs it's like teaching kindergarten some days.

I have a small apartment and am raising my mom and niece, but seriously my mom helps a ton with my princess since I'm teaching, and now pen pals once a week. My mom thinks I need to get out and have fun, so she takes my little princess out for grandma trips as she calls them. You should see a 3-year-old and grandma getting their toes done at the nail salon it's adorable.

That's enough about me for now, I want to know something about you. I look forward to learning about you hopefully starting with your name! ☺

Praying for you all and hope to hear from you soon!

Sera

Brian chuckled softly but he realized suddenly he hadn't received any mail since he had been deployed, not his mom or fiancé had written him, it was kind of nice getting a letter, after the first couple of weeks he had stopped listening to the rollcall for mail because he knew he wouldn't have anything. He noticed Kane had read his and went to the supply closet in the hall to get paper and pens. Brian thought he should get a pencil as much as he would screw it up. He wondered what to write, what was appropriate for a pen pal? What age was she? He knew nothing about this girl which made him nervous. He blinked and realized Gryffin was frowning as he stared right back at Brian.

"What?" Gryffin asked confused.

"Dude I'm thinking," Murphy frowned, "This is hard."

"Just think they didn't have any idea about us and they wrote us. Just pretend you are talking to this girl on messenger or something," Kane frowned at them.

Gryffin stood, "I need quiet to write anything."

"Don't forget to get with Chase to get her address," Wolf murmured as Gryffin walked away. Brian decided to try to write before getting the address, if he couldn't find anything to say he was going to wait and see if she would write him again.

Brian focused tuning the others out as he focused on the paper.

Hey,

I'm Brian, everyone calls me by my last name, but I think it will do me some good to remember my first name for a few minutes reading your letters. I guess I will have to keep in touch with you since I have nieces that I haven't seen in forever and one of my friends here has a goddaughter and asks me tons of questions. I don't live in the same area as my nieces, but I do visit often enough (I just got to remember not to turn them into tomboys). I can imagine grandma and your princess having fun. I couldn't be a teacher, it takes a special person to be a teacher and a special needs teacher, God you must be an angel to do that! I always feel so inadequate to even talk to them. I have a special needs cousin who is super smart in math but he's different, it doesn't mean I don't love him but it's hard to find something to talk about because if we talk math or building things, I'm way over my head and he's in his element, but we talk sports he is bored.

I do like football and basketball. I definitely like to hunt, and fishing is a favorite past time, but we don't have any time for that here. I used to spend a week camping and fishing, best thing I did all year. So, as you can tell I need some help with my nieces because I'm sure I can make them tomboys, but I need to learn more stuff girls will like!

I love to cook, and eating military food is not my favorite time of day. I want a steak so bad I could sell my soul to get one! We try to add seasonings to the MREs but those are in short supply nowadays.

Tell your brother that he needs to build you a house, so he has experience for when he wants to build his own and being in a smaller town, he'd have a lot of work building homes until he finds that perfect job for bridges. Besides he has a niece to take care of too now and she needs a nice castle in a tree and

Letters from Home

it needs to be sturdy. Don't let the other pen pal help…I think her name was Alira or something?

Well Sera, I hope I can call you Sera, it is a pleasure to get a letter from you and I hope to hear from you soon. We are going to have a blackout next month so if you don't hear back just number your letters from here on out, so I know if I miss one and when we can communicate, I will write back when I can.

Keep praying too, our platoon has lost a lot in the last few months and we need all the prayer we can get. Tell your other pen pals to keep writing no matter if they write back or not, they need encouragement even if they don't admit it.

Sincerely blessed,

Brian

Brian thought that worked well, he knew Mercer may not write back but he needed a distraction just like Brian did and when he finished writing the letter he ran to supper with the guys and afterward went to get the address from Chase.

Mercer had just left his office when Brian tapped at the door, Brian asked for the address and Scout nodded to come in. Brian glanced over his shoulder to see if Mercer was out of sight and hearing distance, "He's not going to write back, is he?"

"He said he didn't have anything to say," Scout shrugged, "Maybe once he gets used to the letters he may."

"I told my pen pal to tell the others to continue to write no matter if they write back or not," Brian shrugged, "I'm worried about him, he hasn't really talked to anyone since Johnny passed."

"I know," Scout nodded.

Letters from Home

Brian wrote the address and hesitated, "Who are these girls anyway?"

"Girls from Elizabethtown Tennessee," Scout shrugged, "A couple of the guys in our Platoon are from there and know them."

Brian nodded, "Goodnight, sir."

"Night, Murphy."

Skye was early headed to her internship at the hospital, it was her summer break and she hadn't slept well the night before, her grandpa was sick with the stomach flu and she had been doing a lot of work around the house, Scout and Johnny called to check on her all the time and didn't remember they were in a different time zone and it was super late when they called. Skye saw a sign where Miller's market used to be, it said CoffeeZ. She swung in to get a latte since she had time. She needed caffeine. Skye walked in to fresh donuts smell and coffee. She stood behind Rashel's dad to wait their turn; he was heading to the fields and wanted coffee from what he said.

"Have you met Zaidee?" he asked quietly.

"No who is she?" Skye asked watching the dark haired and blue-eyed girl working fast behind the counter.

"She just moved here about three months ago and started up the shop. It's an amazing shop and Rashel likes her. They went out for drinks a few weeks ago with the girls. She seems to be loving the small town feel here."

Letters from Home

"That's good, I will have to get to know her soon! I've been busy and haven't had much time for anything lately," Skye sighed.

"How's your grandpa?" he nodded understanding. Rashel had told him they were all going over and seeing Skye and helping where they could when Skye was in school. It was hard on her especially with Johnny and Scout being gone.

"Alright, grandpa is getting better by the day," Skye shrugged.

"Hey Mr. Whelan!" Zaidee smiled when it was his turn, "Your usual for you and Rashel?"

"Yes ma'am, throw in some donuts though because I'm getting hungry smelling them."

"Yes sir!" she smiled.

Skye soon met Zaidee after that and told her she was friends with Rashel and wanted to hang out and get to know her. Zaidee agreed excited to meet someone else her age. "We are going to be fast friends since I'm a klutz and you are a doctor!"

Zaidee ended up stopping by the hospital with a 2nd degree burn on her arm from hot grease splashing her two days later and meeting Skye again. As Zaidee predicted they were fast friends and hung out all the time with the others.

Zaidee was always up super early to open her shop, after four years of great business she could finally hire help, but she was usually always there early in the morning to make sure everything ran smoothly. She had expanded business enough that she was open for lunch as well. She usually stayed open until around 5:30 pm but didn't offer supper. It was more a sandwich shop for lunch since breakfast was until noon. Coffee was her number one seller anyway and she did well for herself. No other coffee shop was in town and she kept the prices low, so people stopped in all the time.

She had planned to write her letter Thursday but when she started cleaning up for the night, she lost track of time and went home and straight to bed. She had deep cleaned the back knowing that Friday she was cutting out early and her employees didn't clean as well as she did, she liked to clean and make sure it was spotless. Friday, she forced herself to sit in a booth and write. She had her favorite Peruvian chanchamayo coffee in front of her and she stared at the sheet of paper.

She started to write but the door dinged, Hannah was up front cleaning and greeted the customer but Zaidee was instantly distracted when she heard Rashel's voice. "I need a cappuccino and a chocolate milk."

"Chocolate milk?" Zaidee asked looking up and noticed Serabeth's niece Evie with her, "Hello Ms. Evie, how are you?"

"Good!" she raced over and scurried into the booth beside Zaidee giving her a hug. Her chipper voice asked what Zaidee was doing and Zaidee explained she was writing a friend. Rashel came over with the chocolate milk and cappuccino sitting down looking tired.

"What's going on, Rashel?" Zaidee asked watching her friend.

"I was up most the night helping dad in the south fields. We have been spraying them and we got in around midnight. Serabeth had to work and her mom had to work this morning,

I am watching Princess Evie here until her Gigi is done at work around noon. Dad is finishing up the field and told me to enjoy time with Evie or get grounded. He thinks I'm still sixteen, but I did need a break. He told me when it's pen pal day I get a vacation day he'd work, and I could run errands, go to the store, and make sure we have food stocked up for the week that way he isn't worried about it and we have it. Between the two of us our farm is slowly getting done it's just busy."

"Have you written your letter yet?" Zaidee nodded worried about Rashel getting enough rest and her dad for that matter. They both worked hard all summer and then all winter practically lived in the woods hunting the winter away.

"I've started it, but I'm seriously worried I have nothing in common with any Marine out there. I mean I'm a farm girl the only fun thing I do is teach my Taekwondo class and hang out with you girls," she sighed.

"And serve the princess," Zaidee grinned as Evie slurped at the chocolate milk.

"She's a highlight too," Rashel smiled, "She helped me feed animals this morning, we took a little nap and then came for some energy."

"What did you feed this morning, Evie?" Zaidee grinned.

Evie told about feeding the different animals, cows, pigs, chickens, horses, and ducks. She loved every minute of it. When they left Zaidee started writing again wondering what the Marine would think that got this letter, wondering if she would have anything in common with hers, knowing Rashel had a point. In a small town they probably didn't have anything in common with these guys and it made her worry too. Skye's mantra was 'Stop worrying about things you can't fix, pray about them and let God take care of everything.' But it was a lot easier said than done.

Hello,

So, I have tried to start this letter at least a hundred times it feels like...I mean talking is fine, but when I am writing to someone I have never met it is beyond hard to do, so I decided to just blabber for a bit. Hopefully you find it amusing and not completely odd. My friends and I decided to write because supporting our troops isn't just about throwing money at charities but reaching our men/women and talking to them.

My name is Zaidee, that's pronounced like Sadie except with a Z at the front. I apologize in advance if I misspell anything I'm used to spell check and Skye says if we are going to be pen pals, we must do it right and paper only. I own and manage a coffee shop which is how I became friends with Skye in the first place. I have a small farmhouse that I rent on the edge of town where I have two dogs and a few chickens. All the pen pals (all seven of us) are meeting once a week to write to you all. We have no idea who we are writing to until we receive something back. We live in a small community in Tennessee and yes, I sound like a hick!

So, I know this is super short but tell me a little about yourself, where you are from, what your name is, and maybe if you have ever lived on a farm...I'm hoping we have something in common!

Praying for you and your platoon, many of the local guys joined and most got into this platoon so if you ask around you might hear some crazy stories (don't believe them!)

I look forward to hearing from you and being pen pals if that's what you want. God bless and Semper Fi!

Zaidee

Quinn Bryant had just walked into the rec room and sat near Murphy watching the Euchre game. Murphy had borrowed his cards to play the game, as he sat, he looked at the cards. The cards were faded, bent, torn, and it was getting to the point where the others knew what you had because they could tell the cards apart now. The ace of spades had a torn left corner and the jack of spades had a crease in the middle. It became harder to play because you could identify what your partner and the other team had in their hands and yet easier to make decisions based on the other hands as well. They needed a new deck of cards, no one else had brought a deck and those in other platoons were unwilling to give up their decks.

Quinn heard James step in and announce there was mail to be handed out. They all listened, and Quinn chuckled when Murphy caught the envelope flying at his face. Quinn was surprised that James dropped his in his hand since Quinn was sitting close enough to hand it over. James liked to keep it entertaining by throwing things.

Quinn had gotten one letter from home since being overseas. His mom had sent him a letter about how proud and worried she was for him. He Skyped and called family, so she didn't feel the need to write again. It was weird to get a letter now.

When Mercer asked about the envelope, he looked at the front again and realized he had the same thing. He wondered what was going on and jumped to his feet a half second behind everyone else since his back was to the door when Scout Chase came in, the platoon commander.

When he read the letter, it made him smile, you could almost imagine how nervous and uncertain this girl was through the letter. Her handwriting wasn't uncertain, but the words

Letters from Home

showed that she was just writing whatever came to mind since she didn't know anything about him.

Kane brought paper and pens and Quinn thought about it, if Zaidee was going to take time out of her day to write to him then he would write back. He stared at the paper for a while, Murphy and Gryffin grumbled at each other but he didn't pay no mind to that, it was easy to ignore the others when he focused.

Hi Zaidee,

My name is Quinn, I've never lived on a farm, but I live in a small town in Kentucky, so I sound like a hick too! Thank you for the letter and prayers, it makes me smile knowing I'm not the only one praying around here.

I have a dog at home, it's a basset hound named Dude, real creative I know... My dad is taking care of him for me. I think I miss his bark the most, half the time I was home I was yelling to shut up but now I miss it and his big ears.

I love coffee, we are stuck with mostly water, I haven't had coffee in forever! I like energy mixes and sweet tea. What made you decide to become a coffee shop owner?

I like playing cards, my deck is about shot here but it's fun with the guys to play different games, as far as sports I'm a wrestling guy. I can watch football, but I don't have a favorite team. I like to swim, kickboxing, and hunting. I like to fish but not as much as hunting, there is something about waiting for a deer and the risk of it seeing you first. Fish it just depends on how hungry they are and if you got the right bait.

Sorry it's short, I'm running out of ideas here... Thanks again, I needed it!

Quinn

Letters from Home

Quinn went the next morning to get the address, Scout was busy reading reports and didn't say much but told him that a few of the others hadn't come to get an address but he would leave it out for them in case he was busy to let them know it was in the red folder at the edge of his desk. Quinn nodded and let all six guys know that's where they could find it if they needed it. All of them except Mercer nodded, he was back in his usual spot tossing the ball in the air. Quinn wondered if he would ever come back around.

As soon as Skye had asked them to write they all agreed, Rashel worried that it wasn't going to work as well as Scout thought. Scout always had ideas that sometimes didn't pan out. With Johnny gone she thought that Skye needed more distractions and agreed since everyone else did. They all thought it was a good idea. Rashel just worried that she wouldn't have anything to write about after the first two or three letters.

Rashel tried to write late one night but fell asleep, between trying to get the fields done and feeding all the animals. She would walk in around 11 and be up before dawn at around 4am. She tried to write a few separate times as she went out with her dad to have a fast lunch, writing in the truck, not liking it, and crumpling it into a ball. Her dad chuckled knowing she was trying.

"I don't know if I can do this, dad, I don't know anything about the Marines. The only ones I know are from town and the two I knew the most is Scout and Johnny. I'm a small-town girl that lives on a farm. I'm not anything special."

"You are to me. Besides if you mean interesting people like a pop singer or somethin' like that, I don't see them writing to

Letters from Home 66

Marines. It doesn't matter if you are a small-town girl or a farmer, you symbolize America, a piece of home, and right now that's what this Marine probably needs. They are in high stress situations, they see a completely different culture than ours, and a different language. The only thing they get is media, Facebook, and only when they can have free time. You are giving them something they can hold onto anytime, anywhere to read and remember home."

"I might need some help dad," she sighed, "I don't know the first thing about writing to a complete stranger."

"I'm sure you will think of something sweetie," he chuckled.

They saw Serabeth waving them down, the school closed at noon, so she was headed back home. Rashel's dad stopped as Rashel rolled down the window of the old truck.

"Hey Sera, what's up?" she smiled.

"Mom was told she has a meeting at work tomorrow morning. I need a babysitter until I can get off work. I was wondering if you could help me out. She couldn't stop talking about going to the farm and feeding everything last time. If not, I can ask Zaidee," Sera looked worried.

"Tomorrow you all are going to Skye's to write and meet right?" her dad asked.

"Yes, sir," Sera nodded.

"Rashel can watch her and feed the animals. I'll finish up the field to the South and we will start on the West field Saturday," he murmured.

"Are you sure, there's a lot left dad," Rashel frowned.

"I'm sure, we need to have Roger look at your sprayer tomorrow," he nodded.

She nodded, "If you are sure."

"I am," he grinned, "I want to see Princess Evie."

Rashel shook her head, "Dad says it reminds him of when I was little."

"That's sweet," Sera smiled, "Well I won't hold you up, I will drop her by at 7 if that's alright?"

"Yeah, that's fine," Rashel nodded.

They ate and went back to work; Rashel fell into bed late that night trying to get more done before going home. Her dad was already asleep by the time she got home. She left enough for him to easily finish the next day without her. When her alarm went off at 6, she rolled out of bed and got Evie's muck boots ready. She had bought them after nearly ruining her tennis shoes the last visit. She got dressed and put her own muck boots on before hearing the door.

"Morning Sera," she flashed a smile as she finished tying off her French braid. Evie bounced, "Are we going to feed the pigs first?"

Sera grinned, "Thanks Rashel!"

"No problem," Rashel smiled and pulled the tiny boots off the floor and held them up. They had flowers and lady bugs on them. Evie squealed, "YAY!"

Evie looked at Sera, "Look what Aunt Rashel got me!"

"I see that sweetie!" Sera smiled, "What do you tell her?"

"Thank you!" she smiled and Rashel motioned to sit on the bench.

"How much was that?" Sera asked softly as Evie kicked off her shoes and Rashel put the boots on her.

Letters from Home

"Hey if she comes over these boots are cheaper than her shoes I nearly ruined last time," Rashel smiled, "Besides if Evie comes over again, she has boots here just to feed Mr. Wilber and Ms. Charlotte."

"I thought you were…um…you know," Sera raised an eyebrow meaning slaughter the pigs.

"Oh right, Mr. Wilber and Ms. Charlotte lost a *lot* of weight Evie. They look so small."

"How did they lose all that weight?" Evie asked confused.

"They went to the gym," Rashel was completely serious and Sera fought a smile.

"Alright give me a hug, I got to go to school, Evie."

"Bye love you!" Evie hugged her, "I love these boots!"

"They look good on you," Sera smiled, "Thank you Rashel."

"Anytime."

Rashel let Evie feed the animals, cleaned her up and took a nap with her, woke earlier than Evie did and started writing the letter. She decided they needed a snack and coffee to get through the rest of the day. Rashel had a car seat she kept just in case she had to run errands and kept Evie. All Serabeth's friends shared the car seat since they all helped out. Rashel had Evie the last few times. Sera would pick up the extra car seat if someone else watched Evie.

After seeing Zaidee for a few minutes and getting food before leaving they went home to find her dad there, Roger was looking over both tractors and Evie ran to him, "Uncle Phil!"

"Hey Princess!" he grinned, "How is my favorite curly haired beauty?"

"Good! Look what Aunt Rashel gave me! Don't you like my boots?"

"They are fit for a princess!" he spun her around with a grin, "Did Aunt Rashel tell you she was grounded?"

"She's grounded?" Evie's eyes went wide in shock.

"She stayed up way too late last night!" he frowned at Rashel and Rashel laughed, "We both needed a break today, dad."

"True," he sighed, "Alright you are ungrounded this time young lady."

Evie giggled, "What next?"

"How about we go fishing?" Phil asked her.

"Yay!" she smiled and clapped her hands. Rashel cocked her head and frowned.

"Aunt Rashel has a letter to write," he winked at Rashel and Evie nodded, "Aunt Sera had to write one too."

Rashel went in and sat down and stared at what she had already written. She stared at it for at least an hour before Sera came back to pick Evie up. Changing out of the boots was a fight because she wanted to keep them and wear them home. Rashel put them up and went back to the table. Her dad made sandwiches for lunch and sat across from her. It was about an hour before she was supposed to be at Skye's that she finally started writing again.

Hello,

My name is Rashel. My friend Skye asked me to write for a pen pal. I was kind of worried because I have no idea how to start a letter to someone I don't know. I can talk to anyone face to face but it's harder to write. We had talked a few months ago about supporting our Marines or troops in general better. To do more than just watch the news like everyone else.

I'm an only child; I have four cousins all in the military in different branches. I work with dad on the farm, we are growing corn and beans this year and we have a herd of cows, pigs, chickens, and ducks. I'm expecting three calves in the next month. It's still fighting to break into summer; rain has kept us out of the fields here lately which irritates my dad more than anything because we can't spray for weeds.

I just babysat for my friend; we call the little girl Princess Evie. She's 3 years old and she absolutely loves feeding the animals. Her eyes lit up when I bought her muck boots and you should have seen my friend's eyes when she realized we had…retired the pigs and how I was going to explain that they were gone. We had bought two new pigs that were semi big for their age and I had to explain to Evie that the pigs went to a gym and lost a bunch of weight and were super small now. I keep the same names now that I help babysit to keep from her getting upset. ☺

I hope that made you smile it might make it even funnier that their names are Mr. Wilber and Ms. Charlotte! I'm not sure what to say other than I'm excited to hear back and make a new friend. I'm not sure what to expect so I'll let you tell me what you need or want out of this pen pal experience. We might not have anything in common, but I hope we do. I hope you have a blessed day and we're praying for you.

Rashel.

Zane Wolf was sitting playing cards with a few of the guys. He could tell what his partner had since the cards were old and falling apart. He could tell he wanted to make Spades trump and grinned when Quinn groaned softly, "I was afraid of that."

"It helps I know all the cards in your hand, Quinn," Zane gave his signature wolfish grin.

"Sure, but do you know how I will lead?" Quinn asked leading with Ace of hearts knowing Zane would have to follow suit. Zane shook his head, that was the problem, you make it trump but the other team knew exactly what you had so it was practically worthless to play but it gave him something to distract himself. He was homesick and didn't hear from his parents often. His little brother was in his senior year and headed to the Navy after that. He wasn't sure if he wanted to go into the Marines or work toward becoming a Seal. Zane missed them all, his older sister was married and busy with twin boys and another on the way…although he had a feeling it was a girl this time.

James came in and said, "Mail is here, pay attention people!"

Zane didn't listen, still playing cards, he heard Murphy's name and saw Murphy glance up and catch the envelope an inch from his forehead.

"Nice catch," Zane laughed softly.

A few seconds later James called his name. Wolf turned and tried to catch the letter one handed and juggled it for a few moments until catching it between his thigh and hand. By then Mercer was asking about the envelopes with just their names on it. Zane nearly fell standing when the platoon commander stepped into the rec room. When he sat back down the game was completely forgotten as everyone had letters this time around. They were looking at the letters curiously.

Letters from Home

Zane read the letter, Kane set paper and pens right next to him and he wrote back quickly knowing exactly what to write back. He reminded Gryffin when him and Murphy were mumbling at each other to go to Chase for the return address. When he finished, he went in search of an envelope. He set it next to his kit and went to chow.

The next day one of the guys told them that Chase was leaving the return addresses in a red folder. He remembered the letter and went to Chase's office. Tapping at the door he found it empty. He sat at the chair and copied the address and jerked up when the door opened. He saluted, and Chase looked slightly surprised to find the prankster there.

"Wolf," he nodded, "I take it you came for the addresses?"

"Sorry sir, I should have waited for you to be here," he nodded.

"As long as my chair is still together, I'm alright with your visit," Scout raised an eyebrow and Zane colored a bit at the joke.

"I know better than to mess with your chair sir," Zane murmured.

"Good," Scout smirked, "Did you get the address?"

"Aye, sir," he nodded.

"Did you enjoy the letter?" Scout watched him.

"Yes sir," Zane nodded, "I think it will be good for all of us to get some distractions."

"I do too," he nodded, "If you have any questions about the pen pals let me or your squad leader know."

"Yes, sir," he nodded, "Have a good day sir."

"You too, Wolf," Scout grinned as Zane left not seeing it.

Hey Rashel,

My name is Zane Wolf, please call me Zane, I get called Wolf all the time and mostly because I like to play pranks sometimes. (I will deny it if you tell on me!) We have 3 squads in our platoon and sometimes we play pranks on each other. So definitely call me Zane, Wolf is usually called when I'm in trouble.

It's really cool that you help your dad on the farm, I've never set foot on a farm before mainly because I was a military brat and lived on some base until I was old enough to go to the Marines. It's the only family I know although I do have a Goddaughter, I haven't met that's about the same age as the little girl you babysat. I might need to take notes on how to handle that for when I get home... I've only ever lived on bases so if I went to a farm, I'd be like...what the what???

I was raised on base; my parents signed me up for archery and boy scouts growing up. So, I'm good at hunting and camping. I like watching sports of any kind, I liked to play soccer. I want to learn to sail a boat, I liked boats when we lived on the coast, but I have never been in a sail boat.

Sorry it's short, I'm drawing a blank on what else I like, it's like I started writing and my mind went blank. Do you do anything for fun other than farming? Thanks for the letter and the prayers, it's humbling to know you all care enough to reach out to us!

Z.

Laikynn remembered leaving for the city to go to school, she ran into Skye often enough but was basically on her own. Soon she graduated to becoming a veterinarian and the local vet in town begged her to join, Dr. Moss was retiring, and they wanted to fill his place. She was taking over his clients and the other vets refused to do house calls, so she did mostly house visits and came into the office a few times a week to get things done.

Laikynn felt completely blindsided when all of them accepted the assignment to write Marines. She knew nothing about Marines except what she knew from running into the guys that went over with the platoon, but she never asked them about going over she focused on the animals they brought in or called her to their houses for, they never talked about their time, and she knew they didn't like to talk about it. The one time someone asked Scout about it they had been at dinner for Skye's birthday and he ducked his head and forced a smile, "I served my country and I'm glad to be home."

It took everything for Skye not to go off on the guy, he was a young guy and didn't know, and Scout knew it would happen often enough, so he calmed his cousin down. Skye finally relented and sighed, "It's obvious you don't want to talk about it. Where is Johnny? He's late!"

"He said he had to pick up a special package," Laikynn shook her head, "And no I don't know what it is either."

Johnny walked in with the rest of the girls Skye considered friends and grinned, "I wouldn't be late if they could finish their makeup in the car next time!"

Skye squealed and gave everyone a hug, excited they all could make it. Johnny raised his arms, "What about your favorite man!"

"You better watch it you might just become her Maid of Honor you keep it up," Laikynn grinned.

"Oh God! Please don't do that to me, I swear I will spoil you rotten as long as you never ask that of me. Besides I have a guy in store for her and I'd be the best man," he turned to Laikynn with a wink.

Laikynn thought about that day, quizzing him about this guy none of them had met. He wouldn't say a word, but Scout turned serious suddenly meeting Skye's eyes, "You would like him, Skye, even I agree to that."

"I don't know about that, I'm not the type a Marine could like. I'm not bleach-bottle blonde and rail thin...I play hard to get and I'm sure to get bored especially if all he talks about is hunting, guns, or fishing like you two!"

Laikynn sat next to Johnny and he showed her a picture on a swear that she couldn't tell Skye anything about him. Laikynn noticed the dark hair and blue eyes, she looked at Johnny and laughed, "Dude, she's not interested introduce me!"

"Is he that cute?" Skye frowned at her. Laikynn had waved her hand as if trying to cool off and flashed a smile, "Just your type, Skye, you'd be an idiot to ignore Johnny."

Johnny had planned to get his friend to visit but Skye had to go to a conference in Florida at the last minute and missed meeting him. None of the girls met him but he spent the week with Scout and Johnny enjoying the quiet farm life and loving every second of it from what Johnny said. Laikynn knew Skye missed Johnny and Scout every day but put a smile on for everyone to think she was fine.

Laikynn thought about her letter as she did a few house calls before heading home. She wrote a little here and there wondering who Scout was giving letters to and if the guy was one of them. She decided to Facebook message him so when he had free time, he could check it if she remembered. Soon Friday came around and she gave her letter to Skye with a smile, "This will be interesting."

"No doubt, Adelina said she was going to start videoing since they haven't had a blackout in a while and I'm sure one is coming up soon."

"If she needs me have her call, I'm rarely in the office anymore. The other doctors love me in the field, I only come once or twice a week for shots and checkups, but they handle that since I take some of their clients in the field when there is an emergency."

"Sounds like you are becoming the popular one over there," Skye grinned as they all ate and talked.

Kevin Hayes sat playing cards as Wolf's partner. He was quiet, always had been but unlike at home where everyone mistook that as lack of confidence and insecurity everyone on base knew he was one of the deadliest fighters there. He was a sixth-degree Black belt and didn't take any crap. He was friends with Wolf after Wolf pranked him and they got into a fight. It ended up in a tight friendship since it was a prank and Hayes…after a week of being angry agreed it was kind of funny but only after swearing never to prank Hayes again.

Kevin was surprised he got mail, his family called or skyped they never took time to send anything through the mail unless it was a special reason like his birthday or something. He studied the envelope and jerked up when the boss came in. He caught his chair before it fell and noticed Mercer was right, there wasn't a return address, as he opened the envelope.

Letters from Home

Hello there,

My name is Laikynn, don't worry half the family still can't pronounce my name right so it's entertaining at family reunions because my parents both pronounce it differently. Mom says it's supposed to be like 'Lie-Kin' but dad says he agreed to 'Lay-kin' so take your pick. Hopefully this letter helps make you smile. So, a little about myself…

I am the middle kid of five. I have two older brothers, a younger brother and sister. One of my brothers went to the Marines, the other Seals so the saying Big Brother is always watching—growing up that was true. I couldn't get away with anything! My younger siblings just graduated high school, they are twins and still figuring out what their next step is now.

I am a vet, so I travel around town and have days where I stay in office to treat all kinds of animals. I mainly see farm animals, but I get some crazy animals come through like snakes, groundhogs, and an African cat from a neighboring zoo. I'm the only on call vet in the county so I get a lot of phone calls for emergencies, mostly birthing problems in middle of the night. Never repetitive so that's a plus.

That's a little about myself, I'd like to know about you since this was really hard to write considering we've never met. Praying for you and your platoon, I'm not really sure what exactly to pray for so I'll take prayer requests too. I mostly pray for safety, peace of mind, and rest so add to it if I'm missing something.

If you have trouble coming up with something to write like I did to begin with don't worry it doesn't have to be a book or it can be as thick as a Harry Potter book. I'll write back either way.

I look forward to knowing you,

Letters from Home

Laikynn

Kevin decided to go someplace quiet before trying to write her back. He was surprised a veterinarian would take the time to write him. He was excited but nervous in having someone he had never met to write to as a pen pal. He sat on his bunk and wrote five different letters having trashed the first four before going after the return address. Scout was busy and didn't talk much just politely asked if he liked the letter. He agreed he needed a distraction and left quietly as Scout got another phone call.

Hey Laikynn,

I pronounce it in my head like Lie-kin, a woman birthed you so that's how it is your dad just needs to surrender that battle because he's losing from the sounds of it! So, my name is Kevin Hayes, everyone calls me Hayes here. I want to thank you for your letter, it made my day today. I don't get any mail, so it was a surprise. I am from Virginia; I like and miss the beach. I love playing football and watching the Colts, no I've never been to Indiana, but I do like them (Don't repeat that to my family). I like to fish, and I love four wheelers. I own a four-wheeler and like to play around on dirt tracks I made with a friend on his property.

I think it's cool that you are a vet. I don't have any animals although I love dogs the most, I'm just not home enough to have one. Maybe when I retire, I will get a German Shepherd, they are my favorite, I'd have a male even though everyone tells me they are hyper.

That's about it for now. Thanks again for the prayer and the letter! We need all we can get.

Kevin Hayes

Nadira had a notepad on her desk where she jotted down lines and scratched most of it out until she got a mash of sentences between scribbles. Mr. Jacobi came in with chest pain but otherwise it was slow for the day. She tore the paper off and started rewriting as she had down time. Nurses and doctors came up and talked distracting her, but she finished the letter before the end of her shift. She was supposed to go to Skye's house that afternoon and barely finished her letter. She hated being late for any reason but writing to someone she didn't have a name for was harder than she expected. She reread her letter and shrugged; it was as good as it was going to get.

Hello,

This was tough; I didn't realize how hard it would be to write when I agreed to be a pen pal! I think it's just because I've never written to anyone I haven't met. Letters are so much more personal than emails or social media. I've written this letter close to fifty times at least trying to find the best way to start and make it personal, but I can't. As an ER nurse running the front desk at the hospital it's drilled into us that everything we do, has to make it personal to show we care since we aren't face to face a lot of the time. Not knowing your name makes it hard to make anything personal. So, bear with me since I'm still trying to wrap my head around what to write while I blather on a bit.

I'm Nadira Granger. I moved to Tennessee when I was 18 to go to college and stumbled into this small town and fell in love. I got my degree and started working at the hospital. That's where I met Skye who has rounded all of us up to pen pal with you. Skye is a doctor and I do her charts and data entry for her and three other doctors. Yes, it's kind of boring but when you have two friends working with you it makes your day go by faster. For example, yesterday Alara came flying around the corner of my desk and hid there until Dr. Walsh left. Alara had gotten bored and played a prank on Skye but Dr. Walsh walked into the prank and had blue dye all over his white lab coat. I about died when I saw it. Alara was pretty shaken up since Dr. Walsh does the hiring and firing around the hospital. He asked if I knew who placed the dye pack in the edge of the drawer in the lounge where all the cutlery was; he knew I was fighting to keep a straight face and I couldn't do anything but shake my head. He gave up since everyone knew he was angry and no one saw it, luckily there are no cameras in the lounge, and no one would confess when he was quick to fire people. The cleaning ladies really and truly dislike all the staff. Between rewarding the patients or pranks they have their hands full around the hospital. I keep looking at the ceiling waiting for the little camera orb to pop up any day now!

I'm the oldest of two, my little brother is 12 and he's going through the phase of not speaking to me because I left home to build a career. Mom says he's just bored without me there, but he comes to visit on the weekends so that cheers him up.

Well.... now I am at a loss again. I guess if you want you could let me know your name and a little about yourself (what you like/dislike etc.) We have been praying for your platoon. I hope you have a wonderful day. I look forward to hearing from you.

Nadira

Kane helped with mail occasionally, they took turns passing it out. Today Kane was cleaning his gear, recalibrating his scope on his rifle, busy work to keep his mind occupied. He was missing home and his kids. They were busy with games and keeping his wife busy running five different directions a day. He felt almost guilty that he was overseas and not there to help her get them to games and help with their daily lives, but someone had to pay the bills. Kane knew Martha worked from home and sold houses but with the boys' hockey and other sports they kept her so busy she barely had time to sell anything.

He heard his name and looked up in time to see an envelope sailing toward him. It slid across the table and came to a stop facing away from him. He set his gun down and picked up the letter about the time Scout came through the door. He stood and listened to him before turning back to the envelope. He was surprised as he opened the letter. Most the guys had never received mail that received the mystery letters, so he got paper and pens to sit on the table and everyone congregated around Zane who moved the deck of cards, all of them losing interest in the game.

Kane wrote back but ran out of time, so he cleaned up the rest of his gear, and went to a meeting. After hearing about the blackout coming soon, he wrote more in his room. He thought Nadira and Martha could be friends just from the way the letter was written. He told Martha he had a pen pal from Elizabethtown Tennessee and read Martha the letter. Martha knew he was homesick and needed distracted but didn't have time to do it herself, so she told him to get her contact information to talk to her as well. Kane knew she was busy and just hearing her voice made him want to go home so much

Letters from Home

so he didn't think about why Martha would want the contact information. He reread his letter before putting it into an envelope for sending it in the mail.

Hello Nadira,

My name is Kane McCullough, I am a Fire Squad leader. I live in Chicago but I'm trying to arrange an immediate vacation to our Platoon Commander's house when we are sent home. City life is hard after being deployed here. I find it hilarious that you have to save people from pranks, I have to stop the guys from going too far in their prank wars. They have nicknamed me Dad because I get my dad voice out when they test me.

I have three boys, so I have lots of experience getting the dad voice right. My oldest is Lane, he's 13 years old and into hockey so I get a lot of calls about his games, he's not playing now but Martha—my wife—takes him to the rink to practice. My middle and youngest son seem to want to follow in his footsteps to play hockey. My middle son is Case he's 11 and quiet, more of a bookworm if he's not on the rink. Ezekiel is my youngest and he's 8 and a troublemaker! He's constantly in trouble for something. Martha has her hands full.

I'm happy to get letters, I get phone calls and Skype the family but it's spotty at best. The boys hate to write, and Martha is busy trying to keep them in line, so I don't ask for letters. We are getting ready to go to blackout where we won't get letters or be able to communicate for a while as we work. As soon as it's over I will continue to write but some of your letters may get caught in the hold up. I will try to get the new address to send it too, but our Commander seems to know about the pen pals and you might get it before I do if he has a hand in it!

Keep praying, some of us are homesick and with having !ittle ones I know I get homesick too. A few are getting letters that

Letters from Home

really need it so keep encouraging your fellow pen pals to keep encouraging even if they don't write back because they are going through their own mental battlefields and need all the encouragement they can get. I think it's a blessing you all started writing us. We have months to go and some days seem like a month in itself so we definitely need some inspiration and letters can always be reread.

Thanks again and keep it coming!

Kane

P.S. Although my boys love hockey I'm a football fan and can't listen, read, or get anything football. I'm a Seahawk fan (don't tell anyone in my neighborhood!). I also like jokes and anything to laugh. I told my wife I had a pen pal and she asked for your information to talk to you as well. I am going to ask my commander to get you her number. I don't feel comfortable writing it down on paper being over here and knowing the mail gets driven to the airport off base.

Thanks again!

Kane

Scout was called to his superior's office.

Three hours later he finally made it to his office and found James there. "Yes, James?"

"I hung around to see them read the letters, Mercer frowned a little bit but put the letter away. I'm surprised he didn't just throw it away. Kane chuckled at his and most the others were smiling and writing when I left."

"Good," Scout nodded, making a mental note to let Skye know to keep writing and about the blackout. James nodded and left finding Mercer coming down the hall. James paused and glanced back at Scout seeing a slight nod he left the door open.

"What can I do for you Mercer?" Scout asked.

"Why did I get a letter, sir?" Mercer stood at attention even though Scout offered a seat.

"Someone thought you could use a distraction. Do you plan to write back?"

"Sir did you read the letters?" Mercer frowned.

"They are new pen pals, I reviewed the letters to make sure there wasn't anything offensive," Scout frowned, "Sit down, Mercer, what's wrong?"

Mercer sat at the edge of the seat, not relaxing but needing answers to why some chick he didn't know was writing to him. This girl had no idea who he was and was praying for him? Why? "I'm just confused at why I have a letter. There were a few of us and I've never gotten a letter. Who set this up?"

"That was to be kept private," Scout shrugged, "I think it is a good idea since some might take it the wrong way."

"I don't have anything to say so I don't want to write back. I don't really want letters," Mercer frowned.

"Were they offensive to you?" Scout asked seriously.

"No, sir, I just think they are wasting their time on me," Mercer shook his head and started to stand.

"I'm not going to stop them from writing if that's what they want to do to honor us. Some aren't cut out to fight. The media has been hard on the military branches and what we are doing. These ladies want to show their support and they think a piece of home can help us stay positive. You don't have to read or write back, that is your right and I'm not telling you that you have to do any such thing."

"Yes, sir," Mercer frowned, "But who are they?"

"Girls from Elizabethtown Tennessee, some of our fellow Marines in the Platoon are from the town," Scout shrugged, "Most of them remember the girls, I'm sure. I live there, and you visited Johnny there as well remember."

Mercer left shortly after and Kane came in, "Is this your idea?"

"Nope," Scout shook his head, "I just gave permission."

"Nadira sounds like a good friend," Kane smirked, "We have our fair share of pranks."

"It came in all together, but I have her address," Scout pulled a single sheet out of neatly written addresses with names. Scout hadn't read Skye's letter to him yet but let Kane print the address in a little notepad he kept in his pack.

"Have you heard from your boys?" Scout asked. His wife and kids didn't write they Skyped and called when they could, but it was hard to do since they had spotty service and Skype was delayed so bad it was almost pointless except to see the picture. Scout had seen Kane on the phone and Skype up with their faces frozen on the screen.

"Not for a few weeks, we've been busy and about the time I Skype it's late and they are in bed. Summer just started so Martha said she'd keep them up late one day when I had time. I am getting ready to try them in a bit."

Letters from Home

"Good, I can tell it's been a while, your dad voice gets a little sharper when the guys start up."

"They are starting to get too competitive with the other squads, I got onto James' group last week for rigging the toilets with some Saran wrap. I made them clean it up too. James said there isn't much he can do to punish them since they are already in hell."

"True," Scout sighed, "It's about to get a lot worse."

"I might want to take the kids to visit you when I get home."

"Big city is rough when you first get home," Scout nodded, "I rent a room, but I can ask for visitors."

"You live on a farm, right?" Kane cocked his head.

"It used to be a farm, I think half of it is rented out and there is corn on the east side for this summer. Wheat on the west, it was my grandpa's house until him and his wife passed, and my cousin and I own it."

"How does that work?" Kane smirked.

"I'm never home so it works out perfect," Scout shrugged, "We get along great and she tells me before she does anything to the house. Half the time she has a to-do list for when I get home."

"Keeps you busy," Kane nodded, "I wouldn't mind that too much. I almost dread going home, it's hard to acclimate once we are done here. By the time I get used to it I get called back here."

"I know it," Scout nodded, "I am thinking about retiring in the next few years. Maybe one more deployment and done."

"I'm done after this one," Kane sighed, "My boys need me home."

Scout understood that his boys were still young, and he needed to be home to help Martha with raising them. "I want to meet them soon, Kane, they sound like good boys. I could teach them a thing or two about farming too!"

"They need some good hard work, Martha takes it easy on them," Kane sighed.

Late that night Scout opened his letter and read about Skye's experience with the other girls writing letters. How they were worried that the guys would get the wrong idea that they were writing to find a soulmate or something. He smirked and pulled paper out to start writing her later. He hadn't talked to Skye for a few days but decided to call her early in the morning her time since she was probably still in bed.

Chapter 3
Adelina

Adelina had already started showing up at random places the girls went. The coffee shop was the first place. Adelina had sat at a table with her video camera and recorded Zaidee taking orders and talking to three customers quickly. Zaidee looked at the camera and flashed a smile knowing what was happening. Adelina showed the coffee shop and caught sight of Alara bustling in and getting three coffees. Adelina asked what she was doing.

"Getting some much-needed caffeine!" Alara didn't notice the device in her hand, "I can't talk, I got ten minutes to get food too before I need to get into surgery with Skye."

"What kind of surgery," Adelina asked quickly as she headed to the door.

"C-Section for triplets!" Alara called over her shoulder.

Zaidee yelled after her, "Alara I got food!"

Zaidee ran out the door and handed her a huge bag filled with sandwiches, fresh donuts, and a pie in the bottom having gotten a text from Nadira that Alara was coming. Adelina waited for Zaidee to get back around the counter and asked, "Happen a lot?"

"You have no idea; Skye is one of the first doctors they have hired fresh out of school that was trained for the ER and surgeries of any kind. Dr. Walsh says she's a godsend for our small town. Now I'm going to be slammed with lunch so get going, would you?"

"Sir, yes, sir!" Adelina laughed and Zaidee shook her head muttering that she would think sir indeed. Adelina asked where Laikynn was at and Zaidee called her finding she was at the office. Adelina bustled over there. She was allowed in the back and was recording as she walked through the door. Laikynn had her arm up the hind end of a cow checking the calf with an ultrasound machine she had wrapped around her neck with lenses strapped on her head. The machine went into the rectum and the headset attached from the machine to the lens in front of her eyes showed her the ultrasound in real time. It allowed her to move with the cow and not drag a large computer monitor like doctors used. She heard the man who had brought in the cow talking quietly to someone and glanced around the lenses to find Adelina there, but the fans were so loud, and the cow was in the chute moving as Laikynn worked.

"What do you think of our veterinarian here, Mr. George?" Adelina asked. Mr. George owned a large farm and the cows were like family to him. He was at least once a month for Laikynn coming to visit and loved the on-call option that she now offered to the community. No one understood the difficulty of getting a pregnant cow, giving birth, into a trailer to take to the vet. This one just seemed to be taking too long to give birth.

"Doc Ross is a terrific addition to our little community," he cocked his head at the video camera, "What's this for now Adelina?"

"Sending it to the Marines," she smiled, "I was asked to show a few of their pen pals for when they go on blackouts then they have a little piece of home."

"Don't get any ideas of stealing any hearts out there boys she's not allowed to leave!" he pointed a finger at the camera with a mock angry look, "To be honest Doc here is amazing and when I need her, she is always available. My cow there is about to pop, and the good doc is checking that the baby is alright as well as looking at the way the calf is laying in case it tries to come out backwards. She does more farm animals than anything crazy, she gets cows, horses, donkeys, goats, sheep, chickens, the occasional deer, dogs, cats, snakes, I hear one boy in town has an iguana or something lizard-like."

"It looks gross," Adelina pointed the camera back at the cow.

"She has a glove on, it's not like she does that bare handed," George scoffed, "How is she doc?"

His voice raised over the fans and Laikynn smirked, "Few days still, George. You can't rush a cow she will give birth when she wants to and that's that. I don't see you rushing your wife to have that baby to pop it out any time soon."

"That's because I'm nervous and she's temperamental when she's pregnant!" he laughed.

Laikynn laughed as well, "Well so is this cow! You have chutes at the farm so if she decides to start birthing give me a call and I'll come out to the farm to help her out then alright?"

"Sounds good doc! What do I owe ya?"

"Nothing yet, but if you call me at 3am I won't be so nice. I have a surgery waiting for me inside so are you good here?"

"Yes ma'am," he nodded seeing the gates were set to lead back to the trailer and she slipped the glove off and left it around the end of the machine that looked like a fist sized pill on the end of a wire. Adelina watched her set it in the sink back there and take the machine off before seeing Adelina's hands were full of the camcorder device.

"Don't show them that!" she shook her head, "For real I'm sure they don't want to see me in coveralls with my arm shoved up the butthole of a cow!"

"This is Laikynn Ross, veterinarian in E-town," Adelina laughed as she unzipped the full-length coveralls and stepped out of them. She motioned in.

Letters from Home

"I might as well show you my work space too," she shook her head, "I am here a few days a week, most the time I go to the farms, so the farmers can work and not have to make the trip. That was one of my patients back there about to calf."

"What's the best part of your job?" Adelina asked.

"I'll call you to show you in a few days," Laikynn smiled and motioned her around to show everything and met Adelina's eyes, "Ask away because I can see the questions about to fall out your mouth, Adelina."

"Well," Adelina glanced at the camera, "This is for when they can't get letters so what would you tell them?"

"We just started writing to a few of you in the Platoon. If you wonder how everyone is at home just know they are fine and knowing you can't talk about why there is a blackout or what you are doing has them praying and worrying more about you. I'm sure they are watching TV, if they are kids, they are staying up way too late because it's summer and they know mom is distracted thinking about you. We are all praying for you to have safe travels, and rest.

"We pray for endurance as you work long hours and if we could send full home cooked meals we totally would. We may not know all you guys, we may just know one, but you are a unit and closer than brothers and we pray for all of you as we do the ones we know. I know six just from our little town and that's six families praying, not to mention those I don't know from other parts of America. You have a support system you don't even see, and if you need reminders, I'm sure as soon as this blackout is over with that any of us here will remind you of that. Don't worry about us, those of you that deployed together from the same city or town, the family you have there are connected to each other, and if you were the only one deployed the other families have reached out to them as well."

Letters from Home

Adelina hit stop and nodded, "That's good, I'm going to go find Serabeth. She is doing summer school at the high school."

"Have fun," Laikynn nodded.

Adelina went to the school and visited Serabeth, showing only Sera through the window before stopping, her video died before she could really do more, and she had to get permission from the parents to record the kids first and she was waiting on the principal to get permission for her. She went to the hospital to talk to Dr. Walsh about recording in the building. She promised to cut out any patients and he frowned.

"Doctor Walsh, I can let you approve the video and I will sign whatever paperwork you need," she promised.

"Fine," he agreed, "When will it be done?"

"I have three more days of recording and then I'm going to be ready to come back and let you watch it," she met his gaze waiting for him.

"Alright," he agreed.

"I'll be here tomorrow, I will be mainly recording Dr. Hamilton, Alara Martin, and Nadira Granger," she nodded.

"Alright," he nodded.

"If I do have any patients and I ask their permission to keep them in the video I will get it in writing. Anything you see on the video that is caught by accident any errors or anything wouldn't be punished right?"

"I'll agree to it," he frowned, "Like what?"

"I don't know I just don't want to get them in trouble if I catch something you find wrong," Adelina watched him.

"I promise," he nodded.

She came back the next day catching Nadira sitting at the desk in front of the ER. "I have an emergency; I have to record and edit this before you all send letters again!"

She had said it fast and hurriedly making Nadira stand fast hearing she had an emergency, "Adelina! Don't you scare me!"

"Alright mom!" she giggled, "I got permission to video in the hospital!"

"Don't yell sweetie," Nadira shook her head.

"So, tell us a little about what you do," she checked the angle of the camera as Nadira sat back down and smiled and shook her head.

"I'm the front secretary at the hospital. If you have an emergency, I'm the first one to assist you. If it's not critical I do have you fill out paperwork," Nadira held up a stack of papers on a clipboard.

"Ugh, I hate paperwork it takes forever," Adelina complained.

"Exactly so if it is an emergency, I get them straight back immediately and sometimes have to take over for the EMT. At that point I transition to Alara, she takes over and I come back to my position and anyone that came in with them would fill out the paperwork. Let me page Alara."

"Thanks!" Adelina smiled.

Adelina waited for the doors to open, idly recording the waiting area to the left and right, with the dark blue cushioned chairs, the white walls, and floors. The ceiling was glass so it was sunny today. Florescent lights hung strategically so as not to hang under the glass ceiling but the metal beams. As she slowly spun around, she found Alara standing there with her hands in her pockets. She had her hair up and makeup done just like yesterday, but she was smiling. She jerked her head, "Hurry!"

Adelina frowned, "What?"

"Skye is about to do something, and we want to show our friends!" she motioned and turned racing around the corner. Adelina ran holding the camera as level as possible as she rounded the corner and went into the lounge. She found a little girl with tearstains on her face. Skye smiled squatting next to the girl. They explained quickly what the video was for and the mom agreed to videoing her daughter. Adelina recorded Skye holding an individually wrapped peep in her hand. She looked at the little girl.

"So, I told you if you were good and took that shot like a big girl I'd show you a surprise, didn't I?" she asked seriously.

"Yes," the girl nodded staring at the peep.

"These are special peeps; only really good patients get them, and they only work in the hospital. They are made just for special occasions just like this. Are you ready?" Skye asked unwrapping the peep and sitting it on a plate.

"Yes!" the little girl watched confused.

"Do you want to eat it later or do you want to see how big it will get?" Skye asked first.

"How big it will get," she realized it was going to get bigger. Skye grinned and glanced at Alara; Adelina stood at the edge of the room to get Alara standing at the door watching for anyone passing by. Skye opened the microwave and pulled a chair up. Adelina moved closer to see the microwave and the little girl's curious face. Skye pressed the button and slowly the peep expanded and fell over and made a noise and peep exploded everywhere. Skye laughed as the little girl jerked and squealed with delight.

Letters from Home

"Just remember, do not try that at home, the peeps won't do it and will break the microwave at home alright? These are special peeps. You promise?"

"I promise!" she smiled, "Can I get another shot to see another one?"

Skye laughed, "No, ma'am, you got all your shots maybe next year when you go to first grade alright?"

"Okay!" she hugged Skye and they left. Alara opened the microwave and tossed the peep. She motioned for Adelina to follow her. They started to leave, and Adelina glanced back to see the cleaning lady, she recorded the lady as Alara stopped to look back. Adelina caught the shock on Alara's face and she looked at Adelina and whispered, "Run!"

Adelina jogged to the corner and Alara ditched her and went toward the doors to the ER where Skye was filling papers out. Adelina caught the cleaning lady coming out glancing around and calling, "Who exploded a peep in the microwave again?"

Adelina had knelt and only held the camera around the corner, so the lady hadn't noticed when she first looked around, but she caught the camera sticking around the corner and stepped toward it, "Who is that? Come here, if you exploded the peep so help me!"

Adelina ran toward Skye and said, "The cleaning lady caught me, I need to hide!"

She was still recording and pointed back down the hall but Nadira opened the door and Adelina got under the desk and flashed the camera to Nadira who smirked, "This happens a lot, Adelina. Alara finds her way down there a few times too."

Nadira took the camera and set it in her lap showing Adelina crammed into the small space left under her desk. She heard the cleaning lady, "Dr. Hamilton did you see someone with a camera come this way?"

Adelina seen Nadira glance down and Adelina shook her head and put a finger to her lips and then made a pleading look with her hands clasped in front of her.

"We haven't Joyce, what's wrong?" Skye asked seriously, Nadira angled the camera up to show Skye and Alara standing facing the cleaning lady who was out of sight of the camera.

"A peep was exploded in the microwave, this happens at least once a week, I don't understand why they do that!" the lady shook her head, "I mean we are adults around here, why would they do that?"

"Maybe it's for a patient or something," Alara offered, "I will help clean it up if you want?"

"No, it's not you, I'll get it but I'm going to leave wipes there for whoever it is to clean their own mess!"

"Yes, ma'am, I'll pass the word along."

Alara was fighting a smile and Skye had turned around to sign her name and bit her lip to keep from laughing. They both waited until she was gone to laugh softly and Nadira turned the camera to Adelina, "So Adelina, what do you think of the staff at our beautiful hospital?"

"They are cool, and I'd like to get my camera back the battery doesn't last long!" Adelina grinned crawling out and back around to the front of the desk and offering a hand for the camera.

"Oh alright," Nadira handed it back.

"Does that happen often?" Adelina asked seriously.

"Only a few times a week but normally Alara ends up under my desk," Nadira said seriously. Alara shook her head, "That's only if Dr. Walsh is involved!"

Adelina saw Skye laugh then and caught it on camera with Alara grinning, "We have to have some innocent fun too."

"So, say hello to the guys."

"Hey guys! We know you miss your letters and mail from home. This is to tie you over with the order to wait until you really need it. We don't really know what exactly is going on over there, we have our orders to cheer you up and if this didn't make you at least smile then I think we will have to do something extravagant. So be expecting a few videos and maybe a care package or two from us here in E-town."

"Back to work ladies," Adelina waved, and they waved back, and she turned it off. She explained she was going to work on it and that Dr. Walsh had to approve it. Alara's eyes went wide.

"He promised not to take any action if there was something recorded, he didn't like," Adelina swore, "I will edit out some and let you all view it first alright?"

They agreed, and she left, hiding her camera as she passed Joyce on the way out seeing the searching eyes land on her, she silently thanked God that she brought a big bag to keep her recorder as she smiled and left. She went in search of Rashel and recorded her in a huge tractor from the road and went home to start editing. She went back to town to the local Taekwondo class; she recorded Rashel teaching and went back home. She set the recorder to show her sitting at her desk planning to have a commentary for the first disc.

Late the next day she mass text everyone to view the videos. Most the girls had just gotten their first letters and Adelina got to listen to a few of them. They were super short since they were busy. Skye already knew she wasn't getting a letter, Scout told her he wasn't going to write but to try to make him laugh and gave her some ideas of what he liked but didn't give her the name of the Marine she was writing having told her that if he did it would tell him that whoever talked to her was telling more information about him than what he wanted to tell her and he'd write when he was ready and until then Scout wouldn't give her information.

Nadira demanded that her letter be read aloud for all of them as they ate pizza later. Adelina had brought her recorder with her although she didn't record them reading the letters aloud but hanging out. She caught Rashel about to drink her beer and set it on the counter and recorded it without saying anything just letting the background noise in. Rashel frowned when she stopped. "What was that?"

"I'll show you later," she smiled, "This is for another video later on!"

"Let's see the video," Skye told her.

"After I hear the letters, that's my payment method," Adelina smiled.

They read the letters and she surrendered the DVD.

They had all read the letters that night on the porch from each Marine and Skye had smiled, "Sounds like they liked your letters! We need to write back soon so they have letters back. We might want to write more instead of waiting for their letters, so they get them consistently. The ones we write between just be something funny and explain to them…just funny little diddles or something."

They all agreed it made sense, that way if they were busy, they had letters coming in. Skye put the DVD in the DVD player as

Letters from Home

she talked, and they watched it in surprise. Adelina glanced around at their faces to see shock and awe. "Well, what do you think?"

"It's amazing," Skye nodded, "I think the guys will love it, even if Laikynn has her hand up a rectum."

"I told you not to put it in there!" Laikynn complained.

"Hey, we didn't say you had to be dressed to the hilt and make it look pretty. We are catching you at work not on vacation alright?" Adelina scowled at her.

"Fine," she gave up, "But fair warn me next time you plan to do something for a video."

Adelina shrugged, "Maybe."

Chapter 4
Scout

Scout received a large envelope from the mail runner. He put the rest of the mail in order and opened his mail. DVD cases were rubber banded together and he frowned seeing them, it had a sticky note to read Skye's letter. He glanced at the letters and found Skye's letter to him.

Hey Cousin!

It has been a fast week; between surgeries and office visits we came up with a plan for the blackout. Attached you may have already found the DVD cases. These are videos Adelina made for Blackouts. She's going to make them every so often to send to you. These are to give to the whole Platoon when they need a pick-me-up. I labeled the first one, so you can play it first, they are for you. Keep them close alright?

Everyone loved learning about their pen pals. I really wish you would tell me his name though. It's so hard not even knowing his name. Please keep me posted on how they react to the letters if we need to do anything different let me know. Call anytime.

Love you!

Skye

He glanced at Mercer's letter, he noticed they all were short this time around, not very long. Skye's letter was short too.

Hello,

I still don't know your name no matter how much I ask for a name my cousin says you will tell me if you wanted me to know. We have a surprise for you and the platoon for blackout. Hopefully it will make you smile.

Since I don't know anything about you, I will tell you a little about my week. Like I said in the first letter I'm a doctor, so I had a lot of surgeries this week. I delivered triplets via C-section; it was crazy to see all 3 weighing 4lbs each. It's uncommon to have triplets all weighing the exact same amount. All boys and all super cute, they are in NICU doing well we just have to monitor them and the mom.

Alara tried to make a chair following DIY pictures on her phone, needless to say it collapsed before she even sat in it. She said she barely sat in it and it fell apart. She's not one for power tools and anything to do with building is a lost cause with her. She called me yesterday to help fix it, she tried so hard, and in her defense the pictures didn't show all the steps (this time!). Once she tried to make a Juke ball with twine and glue, she set it on her table and it dried to it. She still has a patch where she yanked it off and it took the finish off the table. She asked her pen pal for some of his hobbies for her to try…he suggested sky diving. Guess what she wants all of us to do now? Yeah, sky diving! I'm scared of heights! I don't want to jump out of a perfectly good airplane! But guess what I got talked into doing? Yes, I'm a pushover and we are doing the class this Saturday. I'm nauseous just thinking about it!

I will write you to let you know how the experience is, I hope I don't get sick on the way down, I'm pretty sure the instructor won't want puke in the face…sorry that was graphic but so true!

I hope this finds you well and hopefully gives you a little smile. You don't have to write back if you don't want to, if you want me to stop, please let your CO know to pass it along.

Letters from Home

I thought the following would encourage you since it brings you and the other guys to mind.

Psalms 110:1

The Lord says to my lord: "Sit at my right hand until I make your enemies a footstool for your feet."

Still praying for you all daily. If you need anything let me know, even if you don't want to write just send a list, I can send a care package if that's what you need that's fine.

Sincerely,

Skye

Scout glanced through the other letters seeing some funny stories and some advice, he wasn't sure if he made a good choice with Brian Murphy and Serabeth thinking there was something odd about him pairing them together and he wasn't sure why. He shrugged, maybe it was a blessing in disguise, and he knew Skye prayed for God to guide his hands. He hoped God did because if he did it himself, he didn't want it to be disastrous!

He put the #1 video in the laptop on his desk. He noticed there were three videos. He was surprised to find little Adelina sitting at a desk. He put headphones in to listen. She sat a little fidgety as she hesitated a moment. He remembered her following Skye around when they were younger.

"Hey everyone! This is for the whole platoon so that you all get a little piece of home. Even if Tennessee isn't home to you, it's America and that counts as home. Some of you are pen pals with my friends. They are definitely *not* tech-savvy, so they asked me to help with videos for your blackouts. I guess it means you can't communicate with home or something so I'm going to be sending my spiced-up video letters from home! I'm Adelina, I just turned 18 and planning

Letters from Home 104

to be behind the camera the rest of my life...So I agreed to give you a glimpse of the girls in their daily life. I think it's awesome that you all are pen pals! I get all of you as pen pals in a way," she spread her arms as if including them with a smile, "So if you are tech savvy send me a video of everyone back, priority one! Just kidding!" She giggled, "Alright for real though I had a blast even though I almost got kicked out of half the places I visited this week! I hope you enjoy my video!"

It went black and white words shot across the screen, *Meet Zaidee!*

It was like fast forward through the door and to a booth. Zaidee was at the register, Adelina was talking again, "Zaidee stays busy from dawn to closing. She makes pies, sandwiches, donuts, and several types of coffees. She serves everyone from old man Jones to Alara who races in and out. Watch this, this is amazing service! They have a system for the girls at the hospital. Alara races over to get coffee to pull through the second half of the day at the hospital and Nadira calls ahead to fair warn Zaidee she's coming."

It goes live with the hum of conversation in the background as Adelina goes up to catch the transaction all the way to when she races out the door to deliver triplets and Zaidee racing after her with the bag of food.

Adelina cuts back to her desk, "Zaidee was super busy at work so I'm going to have to send videos of a day off or a day at home for you all to meet them properly. After that I went to visit our local Vet!"

The fast forward to the door and black words stated, *Meet Laikynn!*

She had the conversation with George and showed her using the ultrasound and her arm in the cow. She kept the reprimand

Letters from Home

in it. Adelina came back rolling her eyes, "Seriously doesn't she know I was told to get the real work in there not the look pretty and smile for the camera? Geez!"

The video fast forwarded through the vet office and froze on the smile Laikynn gave after saying you'll have to wait until I call. It went back to Adelina, "I had to wait two days, at 4am I got a phone call saying to go to Mr. George's house now. I will show you the scene I got when I got to the barn."

George had the cow between the gate and fence, three guys held the gate braced as Laikynn had two gloves and chains around two white feet coming out of the uterus. Adelina had it playing as if in the background and he heard the distressed moo from the cow and smiled. She fast forwarded again to show the baby coming out and slowed back down as Laikynn checked the baby and cleared its nose and mouth with her bare fingers. She looked up, her hair a mess not a stitch of makeup on. "You asked me what I liked best about my job, Adelina. Being able to help make them better, to deliver new life, and to see this," Laikynn followed all the guys out of the pen and shut the gate to let the cow loose to see the baby and clean it up. "Some people think it's a gross job, but I love it. Both the mom and baby are safe and happy."

Adelina froze the picture on the baby and the tongue of the cow wrapped halfway across its face and her giggle filled his ears, "Ok so that is pretty cute but seriously this is what a cowlick is for real!"

She appeared again at the desk gently rocking side to side. Adelina had a sneaking smile around the edges of her lips, "So I have to wait to get permission to go into the classroom with Serabeth, but I do have a sneak peek from the window, you can hear her teaching her summer school class. She is a special needs teacher and she is an excellent teacher, since she started at the high school the special needs students have a great learning experience and not thrown in to sink or swim with the rest of us kids. I know it was rough before Serabeth came to our school fresh from college. So here she is!"

Each start was a fast forward to the building and through to where the girls were found. Serabeth didn't notice Adelina at the door with the recorder, Scout could hear her teaching algebra, "What is A? B equals 2 and B-1 is A. What is B?"

"Two!" one called, and Serabeth did a little jig of a dance and clapped her hands, "So what is 2-1?"

"One!" another called.

"Yes!" she grinned, "So if BX2=A what is A?"

"Four?" a small voice asked and Serabeth spun looking for the questioner.

"Who said it?" she asked seriously.

"Matt did," another kid announced.

"Matt did you answer the question?" she looked at the boy out of view.

"Yes," he seemed worried he had said it wrong.

"You earned a gold star for today! You were right!" she smiled.

It faded out on the frozen picture of Serabeth smiling. "So, you've met a few of the pen pals," Adelina was back, "Rashel is a farmer and the only thing I got was a tractor so I'm going to share it, but you will meet her later!"

It flashed to a slow-moving huge tractor and back to Adelina, "Okay for real she has a secret life not a lot of people know except her closest friends, come closer."

Letters from Home

The camera zoomed in and she whispered, "She has a super power, do you want to see?"

She waited and nodded, "Alright let's go!"

Scout was surprised the video was so good, Adelina knew what she was doing, he was surprised to find the Taekwondo building, it fast forwarded like normal now. He found she was the grandmaster and he raised his eyebrows in surprise.

After meeting Rashel, Adelina appeared again and smiled, "Alright so this next bit you will meet the last three of the pen pals. Don't laugh too hard at me because seriously I was scared. For real don't make fun. I don't take it lightly, I thought I was going to get banned from the hospital. Alright enough stalling let's meet Nadira, Alara, and Skyelar—in that order."

Again, seeing the hospital, Nadira jerking to her feet ready for action made him chuckle as she yelled at Adelina for making her panic. Seeing the peep, he laughed, Skye had told him that she did that but seeing the little girl so excited made him smile. They left, and Adelina cut out the bad jerks editing it to freeze seeing the cleaning lady after Alara whispered to run. Adelina wrote over the frozen picture. *We ran to the end of the hall, it wasn't good video, so I cut it out but Alara left me behind. I had to see what happened, so I stopped at the corner to see what she would do next!*

He laughed as she recorded the lady yelling and finding the camera, she left that run in it and even where she raced through the door and straight under the desk. He roared with laughter and paused the video to try and calm down to listen more. He laughed so hard he had tears in his eyes. He calmed down as it cut back to Adelina, "I've never been so scared in my life, I don't know how they can keep straight faces, but walking past her to leave I was trying soooo hard not to look guilty and I didn't even put the peep in the microwave!"

She shook her head and smiled, "So you have met your pen pals, I was told these videos will be given when you need a pick-me-up, so I will try to make these as fast as possible. I hear we have something crazy planned next week and I get to come to video it, I'm kind of scared so I might have to apologize in advance!" she winked, "See ya soon, I'm Adelina Dale, your video master!"

He popped the video out and put the next one in. Adelina was at her desk and she smiled, "Hey y'all! So tonight, the pen pals are getting together to write and socialize. They all stay busy so sometimes it's to finish a letter. Let's see what is going on. They usually meet at Skye's house. Come on, let's see where she's at."

The drive and up the driveway went fast forward like the other video. He smiled, she made it look amazing and at 18 he knew it wasn't easy but she made it look professionally done. She froze it on the house, *First one here!*

She taps at the door and flashes to her own face, "In this small town when you know someone, and you tap at the door and no one answers, and you hear loud music you let yourself in since Skye's home. Let's scare the snot out of her."

The giggle made Scout smile hearing Bon Jovi blaring in the background he smiled more, it was her and Johnny's favorite band. Adelina waited for a moment seeing Skye's back to her dancing and chopping veggies on the counter. Her hair was tossed on top of her head, she had shorts and tank on, and not a stitch of makeup on. She was singing along as loud as she could and was good. Scout smiled as Adelina stayed back and yelled over the music, "SKYELAR!"

Skye spun and raised the knife to the fighting position that Scout had taught her years ago before seeing Adelina there grinning, she put the knife on the counter and bent over shaking her head as Adelina turned down the music. "Adelina! You bout gave me a heart attack! I had a knife in my hand, you can't do something like that to a person!"

"It was funny," Adelina laughed, Skye grinned and shook her head, "You are terrible!"

"So, you dance around the kitchen while making snacks," Adelina smiled, "Give us a tour?"

"I'm barely home but this is the house I grew up in. I have the same room I had growing up. I own it and *beeeeeep*! Stays here too." Adelina beeped it out and it flashed back to her at the desk, "Sorry classified information is beeped out. Skye and someone on your end gave us specific orders. Alright back to the tour."

"This is the kitchen and dining room; this here is the living room. It's not much but it's home. *Beep*! Has a to-do list when he gets home to rewire the living room for more lighting. It's an old farmhouse and needs work. I kind of feel bad putting him to work when he's home but I'm more likely to accidently burn the house down or electrocute myself if I tried to rewire the house. Upstairs is just bedrooms. There are five rooms up there. Sometimes...*he*—you need to beep out the others Adelina, so they won't know."

Over the video it said, *See? Told ya so!*

"Anyway, the extra rooms are for visitors, sometimes friends visiting from out of town, a few Marines arriving home come to visit...I think it's the quiet that helps them. Cities and stuff here are loud and hard to get used to from being over there so my house is open to visitors year-round if they need it. I'm in and out so much I barely notice. I practically live at the hospital, so company is a welcome when I am here. It's a big house so I like a little noise," she winked. "Come outside really quick!"

They stepped outside, and Skye walked up the hill, Adelina followed with the camera. They came to a pond and fields to either side, she put her finger to her lips and the crickets started, Skye whispered, "I'd come out here with you-know-who after his first deployment, he said this was something he missed was the normal farm sounds. I would sit out here with him and my best friend and listen to them talk for hours about anything and everything they were competitive and most the time it ended up both in the pond and somehow me always getting yanked in after them..." Skye seemed to study the pond as if remembering it her eyes shining with withheld tears, "I miss them, but their job is important. Alright enough reminiscing we better get back."

The camera landed on a cold beer and Rashel's voice asking what she was doing, "Just showing them they have a beer waiting on them when they get home."

Rashel chuckled, "I'll keep the frig stocked up then."

It was muted as they had pizza and wrote and talked, laughing and Adelina came back onto the video at her desk again, "Alright so on this video you got to see Skye's house and learn a little more about her. She loves having company with the girls, but she's prepared for when y'all come home too. I got to say we all want to meet you guys now that we are having fun and learning about you. You will have to wait for the next few videos to see the other houses."

The next video was of the rest of the houses and little blurbs from the girls about their routine, "Why do you write to your pen pal?" Adelina asked each one and everyone smiled and in different words summed it up to wanting to encourage the

Marines that they do have support from the home front and the Media was negative right now, but they still support them, and it gives them something to look forward to. Nadira looked at the camera and smiled, "My pen pal said it right, his family is super busy, or they hate to write. They want to talk and skype, but letters can be reread. If I can brighten his day by writing and writing sometimes really off the wall stuff that happens in my day like Alara hiding from a doctor under my desk, then so be it!"

Adelina came on the last video and said, "I hope you all like the videos. More to come soon, also I was asked to reiterate to the pen pals and everyone else. If you all need anything whether it's just a post card or Chapstick please feel free to contact them through your higher ups or through the pen pals. God bless, we are praying for you all."

Scout called Skye, hearing the voice of a hurrying doctor. "Working?"

"Yeah, getting ready for surgery, what's up?" she frowned.

"Just opened my letters, getting ready to hand the others out. Nice videos tell Adelina those are amazing!"

"I will," she laughed, "Alright got to go, call later to let me know about the letter to my mystery Marine."

"Yes, ma'am," he grinned.

He paused putting Rashel's letter in an envelope, reading a line that said her dad dumped water on her foot when she fell asleep in her truck late one night trying to keep going to save him from having more work to do. She had finished the field but was too tired to drive home so she kicked her shoes off and fell asleep with her feet out the window. He chuckled; those girls were something else.

Letters from Home

He stood unobtrusively out of sight as the guys got second letters. He liked that they got them all together because they all expected one when their names were called. Mercer frowned when his name was called again. He opened the letter and Scout watched well hidden from everyone's eyesight. Mercer chuckled, a smile for the first time in months appeared on his face. Scout smiled; Skye might just be able to help Mercer. Mercer glanced at the other pen pals and Kane caught his eyes, "Who's your pen pal, Mercer?"

"Her name is Skye," Mercer shrugged.

"You going to write back?" Kane asked.

"I don't have anything to say," Mercer shook his head, "Did your pen pal tell you that Alara has talked them into sky diving?"

"What?" Gryffin jerked up so fast he nearly threw his chair backward.

"Saturday after they wrote to us," Mercer nodded with a grin, "Said her pen pal suggested sky diving among other things. Here read it."

Gryffin rushed over and everyone in the room watched him shake his head, "Oh God."

"Read it out loud!" someone across the room yelled at him.

He read just that portion out loud and glanced at Mercer as everyone talked about their little trip they planned, "Why don't you just write her your name?"

"Just a letter with my name? I have nothing to write back why write at all?" Mercer frowned.

"Maybe to show you appreciate their effort in encouraging us, making us smile?" Gryffin frowned.

Letters from Home

"Don't any of you tell your pen pals about me either," Mercer told all of them, "I'll write when I'm good and ready and not a second beforehand."

"What do you think about her sky diving, Mercer? You think she will get sick?" Kane asked with a grin.

"If she lives through the experience, I'm sure she will tell me what happened," Mercer shook his head, "If she gets sick though I hope they take a picture or something as evidence."

They all laughed at that. Mercer snagged his letter back and folded it carefully, placing it with the first. Not noticing the knowing look Kane watched him with. He laid down tossing a nerf ball in the air and catching it with one hand.

Kane instantly started writing back asking if they went sky diving if they were alright? What happened? That one of them was told about the planned trip and they were all curious how it turned out. What they didn't know was the day they received the letters was the day that the girls took the sky diving class.

Chapter 5
Skydiving

That afternoon they were informed they could jump with an instructor. Adelina had a go-pro video camera attached to her helmet, each girl broke down and got one since they were going to do such a crazy once in a lifetime (at least for Skye) event. Adelina asked to go last so she could have footage of all of them going out and the instructor nodded. Taking off, all of them were nervous, Sera was pale, Skye was green with nerves, and Rashel was bouncing her knee so fast that Adelina thought the turbulence was from her all along. Adelina was excited to have such an adventure. She hoped the go-pro was as good as promised for editing and recording. Each team slowly moved toward the door, girl with instructor behind, and when the door opened the wind was crazy. They all went out each with a panicked scream one after the other, the girls screamed bloody murder at first but once their chute opened, they relaxed a little bit and enjoyed the view.

All screamed loud and long except for Skye who screamed at the start and then held her breath to keep from screaming all the way down.

Adelina went to the edge preparing to jump out and her instructor called, "On three! One, two-"

He pushed them out and they free fell for a while, she noticed Skye hadn't pulled the chute, she pointed, and her instructor cursed not expecting her to hear him. "What's wrong?"

"Her chute didn't open," he explained, "They are going to the secondary. There it is!"

Adelina held the straps a little tighter, "Could we pull our chute now please?"

"Yes, ma'am," he pulled the line and it came out, he didn't hear her sigh of relief. When Adelina landed, she found everyone grinning except for Skye. Adelina raced to her and asked if she was alright, all the girls frowned, "What happened?"

"Never again," Skye choked, shaking, "Your pen pal is insane. I am not doing anything that consists of free falling. No!"

"What happened?" Nadira tugged Skye to her and looked to Adelina.

"The first chute didn't release, they used the secondary," Adelina glanced at the instructors who were checking the parachute. The pull string had snagged and wouldn't open the chute. The girls looked at Skye in amazement, "Oh God!"

"Do you want me to cancel the rock climbing tomorrow?" Alara asked softly watching her. They had all gotten the same weekend off which was rare for them to have two days on the same schedule so they were making the best of it.

"It is inside, right?" Skye asked seriously, "With mats and no chance of going splat?"

"Right," Alara nodded.

"That's fine but you couldn't pay me to base jump," she shook her head, "No."

"I am good with bypassing it too," Alara agreed quickly.

"Good," Skye bent over and tried hard to stop her shaking thinking that her cousin was crazy to do that and jumping out of helicopters. She couldn't do it. She stood suddenly glancing around and walking far away from the others before getting sick. Adelina and the others let her calm down before going out to get something to drink and later on when she had completely calmed down, they stopped for some food.

Adelina went with them to rock climb and Skye did well at it, "That wasn't bad!"

Skye grinned as she kicked off, "I could get used to this!"

Adelina smiled and handed her the recorder, "Here I want to go now."

She went up like she was born to rock climb. They each took a turn and all of them grinned coming down, that was a good experience and all of them agreed they liked it. Skye looked at the camera, "I don't know that I could do a mountain but just indoor with the rocks painted was fun. I've had enough adventure for one weekend thank you very much Gryffin."

Adelina went home late that night and started editing all their different angles, watching each one and listening to what they said. She listened to Skye's to find the instructor telling her he was trying the secondary. She hadn't screamed after the initial jump out of the plane until he said that, "What do you mean?!!!!"

"Primary stalled out," he answered.

"Oh God please let the chute work, I promise I won't even yell at Alara or her pen pal, just make it work. Oh, baby Jesus…"

Whoosh!

"Oh, thank you God! Miracle worker!" she laughed, "Dude you just witnessed a miracle!"

"Yes, ma'am," he chuckled, "For your first time you aren't screaming much."

"I was saving it in case the parachute didn't work," she gave a nervous giggle.

Adelina decided to keep all the footage but not to send it. She did however decide to type in what happened and just before

Letters from Home

Skye got sick, she cut it again, typing: *I guess doctors do get squeamish...heights only though!*

She put her footage of all of them floating around in the sky and landing safely on the ground, having gotten permission to set a recorder on the ground aiming up and her go-pro aiming down. She did keep her pointing finger at Skye's parachute but muted her talking to the instructor. She showed bits of each of the climbing and Skye's comment after her summit of the indoor mount Everest. She made it funny with a little cartoon character with Skye's face and an American flag on top of a mountain with trumpets parading. She cut back to her at her desk, "As you can tell we take pen pals seriously. P.S. it was recommended by someone special on our end...me, go easy on the hobbies we aren't Marines we are a bunch of small-town girls willing to try new adventures but maybe not...*that* adventurous."

She smiled, "Until next time, Letters from Home episode 4 complete."

She had never worked harder in her life to rush these videos. Editing was a fun past time but making them amazing and not cruddy was hard. Her family didn't understand why she fell asleep at her desk or had dark circles under her eyes. It took all five days to edit nine different camera angles and condense them into a seamless video of less than 30 minutes. She barely finished before the meeting at Skye's house. She yelled she was going to Skye's before she rushed the video to Skye's house where they were all relaxing on the front porch. Luckily for Adelina she always had her recorder so caught them on the porch relaxing drinking tea and talking about their adventurous weekend. They all had paper out writing to their pen pals about their experience and Adelina held up the video she just finished editing. They watched it and laughed hysterically, and Skye finally calmed and looked at them all,

"I better call Scout and fair warn him about this one and ask if it's too much to show."

"Put him on speaker phone," Alara said as they went back to the front porch to relax and finish writing.

It rang for a few minutes and Scout answered, "Sorry I was in a meeting."

"Hey, you are on speaker phone with all of us writing letters and listening," Skye told him, "We are going to be sending you another video, we are hoping it gets to you before the blackout."

"Me too," he murmured, "We are almost ready and once we start moving it is blackout from then on."

"We will send it tomorrow morning," Skye promised.

"How was the sky diving?" Scout asked with a chuckle.

"How did you know?" Alara demanded.

"The Pen pals talk," Scout chuckled, "I also read it when I glanced through your letters. I won't be reading every single one, but they are all very good and just what the doc ordered around here. I can see a change already in the seven you write. They are happier."

"Even Mystery Marine?" Skye asked.

"Even him. He actually smiled today when he read your letter, you are doing amazing, keep up the excellent work. I haven't seen him smile in almost four months, Skye."

"So, who wrote about it? I thought it was going to be a secret!" Alara complained.

"I did, I didn't think he'd blab," Skye winced.

"Oh, he laughed so hard everyone demanded it be read aloud, the guys were writing you back about it today. Remember ladies to number your letters from here on out. The ones you are writing is #3 I believe."

"Hey, we have video of our experience and Adelina made it again. There is some graphics in there and at the end it explains what happens, but I had some trouble," Skye said.

"What happened?" Scout frowned.

"The primary parachute didn't work, the secondary did," Skye murmured.

"Oh God," he shook his head, "Are you alright? Did you freak out? I know you hate heights!"

"I didn't get sick until I was on the ground," she offered, "Adelina cut out all the extra stuff like him telling me the chute didn't work and me praying and telling the instructor he witnessed a miracle."

"I will review the videos. Is Adelina there?"

"Yes, okay you are on speaker," Skye looked at the eighteen-year-old sitting with her arms around her knees on the porch facing her.

"Girl I could watch your videos any time, they are impressive! Keep them coming, I'm going to do the first one soon if I get the sky diving one, I will wait toward the last day of the blackout and space them out. Like I said keep them coming because they are fun, alright?"

"You got it; we need ideas for what to do though because our everyday life is repetitive for these guys."

"You can figure something out," Scout chuckled.

"I did have an idea from one of the letters I got from Quinn," Zaidee murmured, "He misses his dog, he is from Kentucky somewhere. If we could find out where his dad lives, we could visit and send a video from home from his dad."

"It would be cool to do that for everyone and make it a huge video for the whole platoon," Adelina leaned forward, "But that's a lot of traveling and no information on all the Platoon."

"I can call some people, a lot of these Marines are from the Midwest and don't mind traveling," Skye murmured, "Oh and Nadira Kane's wife wanted to talk to you, I have her number for you."

"How do you have her information?"

"She's my cousin, I'm the Platoon Commander, if anyone in my platoon needs something they contact Skye, she's a point of reference to get to me if needed."

"Scout isn't married, or it would be his wife's job to keep in touch with all the women and family members. So, I have his squad leaders and platoon sergeant's wives' numbers and keep in touch with them, it's a giant pyramid they keep track of around 12 people a piece and I keep track of them, it's more broken down than that though," she shrugged.

"Dang, aren't you busy enough with being a doctor?" Alara asked seriously.

"Coming from the lady that nearly killed me!" Skye scoffed and Alara raised her hands and apologized.

"Alright ladies I have a meeting to get back to, do what you can, they could just video a message and send it to you to piece together if that's what you want to do," Scout murmured and sighed, "Miss you ladies, bye Skye love ya."

"Love you."

Adelina clapped her hands, "Okay so can you get in touch with them all soon?"

"I can call them tonight," Skye nodded.

"Yes!" Adelina smiled and took her recorder out as they all started writing, asking what they missed the most from home. Adelina recorded them each sitting in a circle heads down writing. Some smiling, some serious, Skye wrote quickly and set the letter on the free arm of her chair starting on another letter.

"Skye who are you writing to?" Adelina asked softly.

"I wrote to M&M, to my cousin, this is to Craig. I ran into his sister at the grocery store and he's been on my mind the last two days. When that happens, I usually try to write to them."

"Who's M&M?" Adelina zoomed in on her face.

"The Mystery Marine," she looked at the recorder, "He doesn't write back, and no one will tell me his name, so he has a nickname."

"Couldn't M&M be Mute Marine?" Adelina asked, and Skye laughed, "I don't know that he's mute, he just hasn't wanted to talk. I'm told to continue writing until told otherwise and I take my orders seriously. Besides he ratted us out to the guys about the sky diving trip, so he definitely isn't mute."

"Mysterious Mute?" Adelina smiled.

"I like Mysterious Marine better," Serabeth chimed in, "I'm sure he has his reasons. I mean it's still intimidating to us to write to a bunch of Marines we've never met."

Adelina shrugged not sure how to respond to that. Skye wrote a quick note to Craig and went to a blank piece of paper to write to her mystery man.

Letters from Home

Hello there,

So, I've got a nickname for you. M&M—Mystery Marine, and as you might have guessed since you are getting this letter, I survived the fall from the perfectly good aircraft. I didn't scream but once and no it wasn't from start to finish but when the first parachute didn't work; I didn't puke on anyone but in the grass. You should be proud of me I kept my cool and didn't completely lose it on Alara or her pen pal although I did tell her to make a point that we aren't Marines and to go easy on the hobbies, we are a bunch of small-town girls willing to try new things but not that crazy ever…ever again. Never!

We went rock climbing (indoors). I was way better at that. I have a fear of heights, but the rock wall was better, there were mats at the bottom in case I fell, and I made it to the top. I dubbed the wall Mount Everest because 1. I will never climb the real deal and 2. I probably won't climb any real cliff ever…like never. They need to keep it easy like hunting, fishing, hiking, trying a new sport. Feet firmly on the ground!

We hope this catches you before the blackout. I don't remember if I told you about our surprise, but we sent 3 and with this letter that makes #4 if it makes it in time. No, I'm not going to tell you to ruin the surprise either. I can't believe you told them we went sky diving; it was supposed to be a surprise!

So, for now M&M, I hope you are having a good day and you enjoyed my heart stopping experience with sky diving, and I put two different bible verses at the bottom for you…

Sincerely,

Skye

2 CORINTHIANS 5:7 I will walk by faith even when I cannot see.

Letters from Home

Psalms 50:15 trust me in your times of trouble, and I will rescue you, and you will give me glory.

Some days I just open my bible and start reading. The psalms are from my devotional this morning. I won't stop praying for you and I hope you get some rest before you travel to your next location.

Chapter 6
Skye

Skye had gotten a call from Scout saying he got the fourth DVD and they were preparing to leave the next day. She was already hoping for a short blackout. Some people claimed blackouts lasting over a month and she didn't know if she could survive that long without talking to Scout and knowing he was alright.

The first week went by quickly considering they were contacting everyone to get recordings and everyone was calling Skye to find out what she knew about this blackout. Martha, Kane's wife, called her to vent about the oldest boy's summer school grades and suddenly sighed apologizing for unloading. "It's hard when I don't have him to talk to you know? It's like I must hold it all in until he is available to talk again. I honestly am thinking of making an executive decision to move your way, so I have help while the boys are overseas. The boys would hate not having hockey though."

"I know what you mean, Martha. Call any time, you know that," Skye smiled, "I might come visit you since we are planning to travel to record some families that aren't tech savvy. Adelina isn't allowed to go by herself, so I took vacation in two weeks to help her."

"You need distracted too, it will be good, bring it on, I will make my world-famous pie, and you can tell me if I'm better than your friend Zaidee I have heard so much about."

"Kane talks to you about everything doesn't he," she laughed.

"He's happy to have the distraction and to be honest he needs someone that won't add stress to his life the way I do. I tell him about the bills, orthodontics for Ezekiel our youngest, Lane's grades and attitude problem, and anything that goes wrong with the house. With his pen pal Nadira, he gets easy distraction without added worry. The only one that isn't trouble is Case and I only yell at him to get his nose out of a book and do his chores or homework."

"Nadira was worried sick about writing to the guys because she was scared, she would end up getting hit on," Skye laughed, "She actually likes talking to Kane because he's taken and won't ever hit on her."

"Does she have a boyfriend?" Martha was confused by that.

"No, she got out of a terrible relationship last year and wants nothing to do with guys for a while. The bad part is the guy was in the Army which makes her cringe at the thought of a Marine getting any bright ideas."

"Well, I'm glad someone knows how to match up the pen pals then," Martha laughed, "The first thing Kane said was I hope this girl doesn't get any ideas since I'm happily married."

"Oh geez!" Skye laughed, "We are too busy to get any ideas about anyone."

"Have you been told who you write to yet?" Martha asked trying to act as if she didn't know and failing miserably.

"No, I take it Kane told you that too huh?"

"I can neither confirm nor deny," Martha chuckled, "But seriously keep writing, Kane said he could see a change in attitude already."

"Attitude?" Skye frowned, "Is he one of the ones Scout complains about getting into fights and such?"

"No," Martha glanced outside to check on the kids and switched ears holding her cell phone, "He is depressed and barely speaks unless forced to by superiors."

"I see," she murmured, "Well I have no idea if he even likes my letters, I wrote to tell him I survived the sky diving stunt Gryffin suggested. My first parachute didn't work so I'm sure he got a kick out of that."

"Oh my," she whispered, "That's insane."

"Yeah," Skye scoffed, "I nearly puked on the instructor and what does he say? You aren't screaming much. I told him I was saving it in case both chutes didn't work."

Martha was shocked, "I hope you plan to keep your feet planted because I need you, Skye."

"Definitely, no more adventures like that, hiking only from here on out," Skye laughed.

"So, when should I expect you?" Martha asked.

"Adelina has a list of people we need to see so she's bringing that tonight. Did you get her email?"

"Yeah, I said I am mediocre at cameras and would rather her do it," Martha laughed, "She said she added me to the list."

"Good, I will have her email you the itinerary for me," she smiled, "I have to go back to work, but it was good hearing from you and tell Lane if he isn't good, I'm going to video duck taping him to a chair for bad behavior."

"I'll tell him," Martha chuckled, "I'm about to ground him from the rink until he fixes his problem."

"Everyone deals differently with a family member being away from home, he's probably just missing dad," Skye smiled, "He does need to bring his grades up so if he needs help with science or math give me a call, I'm good at those two subjects. Anything else I can see about a tutor or Adelina to help him out."

"Thanks Skye," Martha was getting choked up, she couldn't ask for a better network of women to keep her sane.

"Don't go crying on me because I'll join you and I have surgery and can't have my eyes burning from wailing alright?" Skye warned and heard her take a deep breathe.

"I'll talk to you later, Skye," she said, and Skye heard her yell at the boys to come in for dinner. She smiled as she hung up.

Vacation came, and they went to Quinn's parents' house first. They were sweet and showed them around. Kane was next living in Chicago. Martha was home and Skye gave her a huge hug as Adelina recorded them. "I'm so glad you came!"

"Me too," Skye smiled, "This must be Ezekiel and Lane. I take it Case is reading somewhere?"

"Yes," she rolled her eyes, "I'm almost to the point of taking the books from him and grounding him from books but then he'd say he can't do his homework. I've tried before he's too smart for me to argue with."

The boys took off to find Case, Adelina grinned, "Sounds like you have your hands full."

"I do, it's nice to meet you Adelina, I wish Nadira could have come with you I so wanted to meet her. She is such a sweet girl. I've called her a few times, so I could stay sane and not strangle a munchkin."

Adelina laughed, "Nadira has that effect on people."

They recorded the family and went to the rink for the boys' game which they won. Adelina recorded it just for Kane. She smiled, "I may have to send him two DVDs."

"We normally celebrate with pizza at their favorite parlor," Martha murmured, "Are you up for that? Do you have to leave soon?"

"We have to leave in about an hour to make it to the next destination. We aren't going to get a lot of sleep on this trip," Skye smiled, "Adelina is cramming so many states it will be a miracle if I make it back on time."

"I've not seen most the states we are going to," Adelina smiled, "I'm glad Skye agreed, or I'd be Skyping people trying to teach them about their cameras."

"Oh Lord!" Martha laughed, "You probably wouldn't even know how to work ours it's so old!"

Adelina giggled as they recorded the boys taking their gear off and heading to the van. Skye drove forever, and Adelina drove a few times, but Skye knew she was nervous on the interstate and Skye's rental car. They stopped at rest stops to sleep for a few hours but otherwise drove straight through until Skye couldn't stand it and pulled into a hotel to sleep. She wanted a shower and a bed to try to sleep. Adelina didn't say much but talked to her about Scout and the girls. They talked about Johnny and how most the guys were all in the same platoon for their first two tours and all of them knew Johnny. She asked about Skye's favorite memories of Johnny and hid that she was recording Skye. She was shocked that Johnny used to swear he'd marry Skye.

"What happened?"

"We went on a single date," Skye laughed remembering how awkward it was for them, "It was like going on a date with your brother. He looked at me in middle of dinner and gave a huffy sigh before saying it wouldn't work. I agreed with him and he asked if that changed anything for us. He was a nervous wreck that it would ruin a great friendship and I laughed at him. Some things would never change with him, I told him I'd always love him just not any more than brotherly love. He was about to go to boot camp with Scout and reminded me that I promised to write them both or he'd call everyone in town to remind me to write them."

"He was serious," Adelina murmured, "Why did he want letters?"

Skye's eyes were misting and she took a steadying breathe, walking down memory lane was hard but Adelina had known Johnny and her were close and was curious. Skye wasn't like some who never wanted to talk about them but to remember the good times. She quickly swiped a tear off her cheek, remembering such a serious moment then but funny now made her miss him even more.

"Grandpa told him about grandma writing him letters while he was in the service and how it helped him get through some rough days. The boys had me swear to write them in front of grandpa, so it was official, and I would never get out of it. I enjoy writing to everyone anyway. There is something almost relaxing about it. Most people would rather text or Skype them but there are times like now where Scout's platoon can't call home, so they have whatever is on them to remember home. Letters are something they can reread any time."

Adelina nodded and pointed to the driver's side, "The ocean!"

"You haven't been to Florida since you were little right?" Skye asked. Secretly she was glad for the distraction, she had to focus and didn't want to cry, she hated to cry, and everyone knew that about her. The sky was bright blue, the ocean a sparkling mass out the left-hand side of the car. The beaches were full of people enjoying the sunshine.

"We went to the Keys, but I don't really remember it," Adelina bounced in her seat.

Skye parked for a minute and took Adelina's camera, "Come on, camera girl."

Adelina laughed and took off for the water. Skye recorded the ocean, "I hope she sends this to you boys; she's only seen the ocean when she was small and barely remembers it. You would have thought she got Christmas early this year."

"Come on, Skye!" Adelina motioned.

They planned to finish with the last family in Texas before heading back home to Tennessee. Skye slept the night away before getting up early and going to work. Adelina called her to review some DVDs she made already. Skye picked them up and took them home. She smiled and called Adelina, "They look amazing."

"I made fliers for the community to know we are sending a care package to the boys. They are giving everything to Zaidee since she's in town."

"Sounds good," Skye nodded, "Spread the DVDs out so the others can watch some as well. I can't watch every single one. These five look amazing though."

"Get some sleep, Skye. I can get someone else to watch them for me," Adelina agreed knowing Skye didn't sleep most the time they travelled. Adelina had fallen asleep in one state and woke up in a different state and new location as Skye drove her from place to place. She knew she missed Scout and worried about him. The other girls agreed to watch the DVDs, and she delivered them as she got them done to Nadira, Zaidee, Laikynn, Serabeth, Alara, and Rashel. Once they were approved, they were given to Skye for safe keeping. Alara went to the post office and explained to Wanda what they planned and Wanda surprised Alara with giving a steep discount on everything they needed, "You just tell them boys we miss them and want to send a little love their way."

They had sent a few family members of other Marines in the Platoon to Skye's house to help address and prepare the boxes.

Letters from Home

Adelina noticed Johnny's mom was there and pulled her aside for a moment. "I don't know if you are interested but we went on this trip to get the recordings of family members who couldn't record themselves. I was talking to Skye about different things and Johnny was brought up. She was telling some funny stories about him and growing up. I recorded it without her knowing and planned to give it to her for her birthday, but I thought you'd want it too. I can burn another DVD if you do."

"I'd love that," she smiled her eyes pooling, "You are such a blessing Adelina."

"To be honest I'm just goofing off," Adelina gave a cheeky smile. It hurt to see her miss her son, she didn't realize how much it meant to her to get a DVD of memories from others.

"Look around, this doesn't look like goofing off to me," she motioned around the full house, "You did this, Adelina, you brought this about to help our boys over there be less homesick. Without you they'd not get anything but pictures and letters and most not even that."

"But it's just a video," Adelina shrugged. She was getting experience, planning to use that to get into college and maybe test out of classes. She knew most the guys in the platoon from town and wanted to give them a piece of home. She was driven when it came to videos, she liked to make them look cool and interesting.

"Look at it this way, you go to a different country where women wear full dresses and the entire population speaks a different language. Every turn is a possible danger to you and your friends. You live every day feeling the stress of never knowing what will happen next. The only time you can talk to family is when they pick up the phone and it's a different time zone, so most families are working or sleeping when you have

Letters from Home

time to call. Skype barely works in some areas, and no one writes letters to you anymore. Suddenly a young lady you never met before sends you a DVD and it's of your family and friends, a snapshot of home and for those precious moments you are back home hearing your dad's voice, your sister's voice, your mom…it's something you can play any time you need to hear their voices. That's a gift they will cherish because a girl they never met wanted to give them a gift from home. I don't call that goofing around."

Adelina looked surprised, "I didn't think of it that way. Skye asked me to make a few DVDs for Scout to share and it kind of got out of hand from there. I go nuts when I get interested in something."

"Well, you do this really well and if you need a reference for anything you let me know."

"Thank you."

"Any time."

Chapter 7
Blackout

Scout had received the fourth DVD the day before the blackout. He watched the video and knew that Adelina pointed to Skye because her chute hadn't worked. He was amazed his cousin took it so well and knew she would never sky dive again. At the end he laughed softly, most were humorous videos and he was happy with the girls' work. Skye had already told him that they reached out to the families and everyone was sending Adelina videos. Some were longer others shorter, so she asked Skye if she could get some help buying DVDs to separate them into individual gifts as well as making two videos of some awesome parts. She had to ask Skye to have them record a little piece of home and to answer one question, if you could tell your Marine what you thought of him what would it be.

They hadn't received letters for nearly a month and a half but continued to write and send letters, so they had a lot of mail when they could get it. Skye had the updated address and got a lot of phone calls from worried families wondering what was going on with their Marine. She explained the blackouts could last a little longer, that some were short. This just was a long one and they would be online any time soon.

Scout and his platoon traversed cross country to their location. They had four separate encounters with hostiles and some of his men were wounded but fine. One encounter was a close call, they were getting hit from three sides, the hill behind them was steep. Scout wasn't sure where his scouts were or if they were dead, he hoped they were alive. He had to find a way out of the situation. Scout saw it was impossible odds.

Scout didn't have time to think about the scouts he had sent out to check the road ahead. They had moved out of the area and around the hill to look around. Mercer was with the scouts, two others were with him, the teams of three was a Marine thing—1 team for Assault, 1 for Support, and 1 for Security. Mercer fell into support most the time but sometimes security as in now when they traveled. They heard shots fifteen minutes after leaving the platoon at the trucks. Mercer tapped Sweet and pointed to the hill separating them from the team. They went up, Sweet watching their six, making sure no one snuck up on them.

"Sweet, there is a drop of three feet, it plateaus out, stay here and watch our six."

"Roger that," Sweet murmured and laid down to keep from being seen.

Mercer and Gryffin slipped down and set up. Mercer couldn't ask for better vantage. He laid down, he remembered to grab his bag before he left, which held more ammo for his rifle. He took in the scene below, one man in a shalwar kameez of matching gray and white ghutra and black egal stood to one side holding a radio. Mercer took out the machine guns, continuing to select his targets strategically. Sweet done the same, both careful to keep an eye on the enemy to make sure no one noticed the plateau where they shot from. The longer they fought the more likely they would have more friends come to the party. Mercer kept an eye on the radio, seeing one or two go after it, he took them down, it was like plutonium so no one could get it. They called a retreat, Mercer held fire when they took off. When they took off Sweet called, they had company, the retreat was a fake, they were coming around to attack from uphill. Mercer took the chance and stood, "Sir!"

Kane happened to swing up to look up him, his gun half way up when he recognized the uniform, "Mercer?"

"Yes, sir, enemy are coming up this hill," he called turning to see how far they are. Sweet took aim at a tire, missed hitting the gas tank, blowing the truck in front, three others hit it and injured plenty of men, Gryffin hit a driver, Mercer took out the machine gun before any shot was taken. Those that could retreat swerved and left.

"Sweet, Gryffin, go now," Mercer held his position. One or two men started for the hill and he shot them. The trucks were running and Kane yelled for him to come on, they were getting out of dodge. Mercer shot twice more and ran down the small trail to the group below. He jumped into a truck and they took off.

"They were retreating except those who didn't have a vehicle, I think we are okay for a bit."

"Keep eyes on," Scout told him, Scout always rode in the front or at the back, where the danger was normally greater.

"Yes sir," Mercer nodded, noticing a bandage on his arm.

It took five days to arrive and another three to set up their area. They were given a tour of the area and settled in quickly before being sent on two missions back-to-back. He noticed exhausted and homesick looks around his men. They had the day off until someone changed their minds, so he had all the squad leaders pull everyone in for a meeting. He heard grumblings as they complained it was a day off. Kane ordered silence just as Scout came into the tent and everyone came to attention.

"As you were," he murmured, "It was brought to my attention that the pen pals sent a surprise before the blackout and gave special orders to only use it when everyone was homesick and needed some encouragement or just a good laugh. Have a seat and enjoy this video."

They all murmured in surprise as Kane put it in and turned the volume up. They watched in shock.

"Hey everyone! This is for the whole platoon so that you all get a little piece of home. Even if Tennessee isn't home to you, it's America and that counts as home. Some of you are pen pals with my friends. They are not tech savvy at all, so they asked me to help with videos for your blackouts. I guess it means you can't communicate home or something so I'm going to be sending my spiced-up video letters from home! I'm Adelina, I just turned 18 and planning to be behind the camera the rest of my life…So I agreed to give you a glimpse of the girls in their daily life. I think it's awesome that you all are pen pals! I get all of you as pen pals in a way so if you are tech savvy send me a video of everyone back, priority one! Just kidding!" She giggled, *"Alright for real though I had a blast even though I almost got kicked out of half the places I visited this week! I hope you enjoy my video!"*

Scout watched from the back of the room, everyone sat still as statues until the end, sometimes chuckling, but mostly sitting, staring in awe at such a well-made video from an 18-year-old girl from Tennessee. Scout saw some take in the background of the video, the people walking and the woods and farmland. Nothing like the desert and just what the doctor ordered for them. When the video ended it was quiet for a moment.

"Those girls went all out," Hayes laughed.

"Could you imagine sticking your arm up a cow's—" everyone laughed.

"Are we going to send a video back?" Gryffin asked with a quiet smile. He thought it was pretty cool to see each girl and have a face to go with the name. The other guys that got letters were sitting close together and they seemed excited about the video…all except Derek Mercer. He looked surprised but was frowning.

"Mercer you good?" Quinn asked softly confused.

Letters from Home

"I remember the coffee shop being a tool shop," he frowned, "That town has changed a little bit."

Mercer had told Scout and Johnny once that he loved the peaceful town, where everyone was friends and they helped each other, so unlike the city where he lived. Johnny had taken him to Scout's house to chill out and fish, it was after the second deployment and he was surprised at how relaxing it was out there.

"You've been there?" Quinn frowned.

"Johnny was from there. I went to stay for a week with him," he met Quinn's eyes, "It's a peaceful small town."

Johnny never said anything about Skye or told him about her only that he had a close friend that he would like Derek to meet. Scout had been there, but it wasn't awkward considering they were best friends and off duty as Scout jokingly put it.

"Alright everyone!" Scout stood in front of them, "We have a few more DVDs so the next day we have free we will watch another."

"Can't we have 1 more today? We have been good, sir," Kane looked like a little kid as he grinned. It had been a hard few days and they were all exhausted and missing home badly, not being able to talk to loved ones made it worse, and Kane was taking it hard. He had caught a few of the guys pulling letters from the girls out and rereading them. He found a notepad on Mercer's cot, but nothing written. Even Derek was having a tough time with it although he never said a word about it. His family never called or sent letters, so Mercer was used to being cut off but the few letters he had received made him miss home. Kane hoped Scout would agree as a few others made agreements softly.

Scout smiled, "One more."

Letters from Home

Scout had the second DVD with him anyway. He knew it was of his house and the pond, he really wanted to watch it and didn't mind sharing with everyone anyway. They watched the second one and Derek looked shocked. Kane noticed he was pale, "Alright Mercer, what is wrong for real?"

Everyone was leaving and talking so no one else noticed, "Nothing, I need some air."

He saw Scout taking off and caught up to him, "Do you have a minute, sir?"

"What is it, Mercer?" Scout met his gaze.

"That's your cousin Skyelar?" he knew it was but wanted to hear it.

"Yes," he stopped and met his gaze, "What is the real question, Mercer."

"Did you put her up to writing to me? Does she know who she is writing to?"

"I have not told her who she is writing, as far as putting her up to writing, no she asked me what would help the men and if they would like letters. The team leads chose who received the letters not me."

Scout stretched the truth some because he was worried for his team, he didn't want them thinking he put Skye up to it (even though he did).

"Why me?" he frowned.

"Ask your team lead, maybe he thought a piece of home would take your mind off what we are doing here."

"Why Skye? Why not any of the others?"

"It was luck of the draw," Scout watched him, "Do you have a problem with Skye writing you?"

"No," he hesitated, "How can she be so positive when she lost him too?"

Mercer remembered Johnny getting letters and telling Mercer that he'd like Skye, she wasn't like the city girls, she was easy going and observant. Skye and Johnny went back to just before middle school. Johnny had told a few stories but Mercer hadn't met the girl his best friend loved like a sister. Knowing Skye was the one and the same girl Johnny talked about.

"It's Skye, she stays busy and helps others, she has moments just like we do."

"Does she know about me?" he frowned.

"Nothing about you except stories Johnny told her, he told her that she would like you but the week you came to visit she was supposed to be home but had to go to Florida for doctor stuff."

"So, Johnny tried to get us to meet?"

"Yeah, a few times but you two were stubborn," Scout smirked, "I have a meeting but come find me later, Derek. It's driving her insane to not know who she is writing."

"I still don't know if I want to write her back, sir," he knew he may be viewed as disrespectful but didn't mean it that way.

"That is up to you," Scout shrugged, "Until you tell me otherwise, I won't make her stop writing either though."

"I think Skyelar is the glue for the pen pals to keep writing and the other guys need the distraction."

Scout nodded staying serious even though it was hard seeing right through Mercer, he enjoyed the letters and didn't want to give them up but made it seem like he was suffering through for everyone else's benefit because the girls would slowly peter out if Skye wasn't involved. "Of course. Find me later, Mercer."

"Yes, sir."

They were called on a mission late that night, taking off to offer support to another division which was behind enemy lines trying to get back. When they got back to their barracks even Scout wanted to see the DVD with Skye in it, he needed to hear her voice. When he came to the rec room, he noticed the DVDs were sitting next to the TV for anyone to watch. He told the ones there to get the others rounded up, he held up the DVD when they asked if it was another mission and they grinned taking off calling for friends and to pass the word that Scout wanted them. Everyone was accounted for and standing in the rec room as he waited. Kane came in with James and Toby the platoon sergeant.

"Anyone want to watch a DVD with me?" he asked with a smirk. They all chuckled and agreed with him. They watched the third one, with all the other pen pal's houses, and the small town. Scout watched it feeling like he was driving down the road seeing the town, Adelina was amazing. It was quiet for a moment and this time Hayes smiled, "Sir have we been good enough for another DVD?"

"Kane in my desk is the last DVD in the bottom drawer on the right-hand side," Scout smirked, "You are in for a treat considering Gryffin told them to try some of his hobbies."

That started a buzz of conversation as they waited for Kane to get the next DVD. Scout had a meeting later that day but had time for one more DVD. They watched it and most the guys hadn't heard how the skydiving lesson went except for the pen pals so most were surprised the primary stalled out on Skye's shoot and everyone laughed at seeing her slightly green complexion as she looked directly in the camera and said, "Never again…NEVER!"

Gryffin shook his head feeling as if she yelled at him not the camera, still shocked these girls would ever try skydiving because he recommended it. When it was over, they all shook their heads and talked quietly. Quinn asked Scout when blackout would be over, and Scout noticed the instant silence.

"I have a meeting this afternoon and I will be asking when we will be out of blackout. Be prepared to have trouble with the wi-fi being slow and be patient since everyone will be wanting to call home. If we have trouble, I can have our team leads set a roster for timed phone calls," he knew some guys fought over the phones since there was a high demand, so he was warning them he wouldn't be nice about it.

They all agreed and went back to whatever they were about to do when he called everyone there. He noticed Mercer was back at his usual spot tossing the nerf ball. He wasn't expecting a fluctuation in mail from the girls but wasn't sure how many letters Skye would have them writing.

He went to his meeting and was told they were cleared and could call home the next day. He called his squad leaders and they all watched him worried they were going to have to deliver unwelcome news to their guys. Scout met Kane's eyes, "Martha will love hearing from you tomorrow."

They all grinned knowing Kane was getting homesick and his dad voice was permanent the last few days. Scout glanced at the others, "Tell your men tomorrow we can call home. I meant what I said about rosters if there is a fight over phones like the last deployment blackout."

"Yes, sir," they took off to tell the others and Scout heard cheering down the hall and chuckled. Late that night they were called on another mission and had the worst fight they had seen since Johnny had passed. Scout had two men in critical condition in the hospital. He was amazed at how long they had been on blackout; it shouldn't have been that long but they kept getting pulled to other missions along the way. A month and a half was too long to go without talking to Skye.

As soon as he knew Skye would be awake, he called her, she answered quickly, "Hello?"

"Hey Skye," he smiled feeling exhausted and ready for home.

"Scout," she sighed, "I thought it would never end, I missed hearing your voice."

"You know I was so happy to have those DVDs, so I could hear your voice," he smiled, "The guys loved it."

"They are all about to have a surprise, I took some vacation time with Adelina and sent a few surprises in the mail," she smiled.

"You sound tired," he frowned.

"You too," she chuckled, "I've got ER for the next two days, I was called in early this morning and had a six-car pileup come in at around 3am. I have done four emergency surgeries and taking a break to eat lunch before a few more tonight. Have you got mail yet today?"

"Not yet," he frowned at the quick change in subject, "Why?"

"The mail man may hate us by the end of the week," she chuckled.

"Why is that?" he heard his email ding and checked it to find an update on his two men they were stable and about to be sent to the states for more surgeries and physical therapy. He had two new men flying in that night to take their positions.

"I told you I have been working with Adelina," she smiled, "I love you, Scout."

"I love you too, are you sure you got to go? I want to talk a bit longer," he sighed.

"Call later and I promise to be full of fun topics and not distracted with seventeen emergency room patients and more than two surgeries this afternoon, Scout I promise," she smiled, "I'm eating, talking, and trying to read reports at the same time."

"Sorry I know you are busy," he sighed.

"Hey, I'm never too busy for you, besides, I miss you and if I could push the surgeries off I would," she saw Alara coming down the hall toward her, "Alara is coming to tell me the next surgery is up though."

"I'll call around six your time?" Scout asked.

"Yeah," she nodded, "Love you."

"Love you," he murmured looking up to find Kane standing there.

"Were you talking to Mercer's pen pal Skye?" Kane smiled.

"He told you?" Scout leaned back rubbing his face missing her already and hardly able to wait for six to come around.

"Yeah, that was a short phone call, you didn't have to end it because I walked through the door, boss."

"No, she had a six-car pileup come into emergency and had surgeries," he shook his head, "You call Martha?"

"Yes, sir," he grinned, "She said next time it's that long she swears all my bosses will have an ear full even the president."

"I agree with her," Scout smirked, "What's up?"

Letters from Home 144

"I got an update on our guys," Kane murmured.

"They are headed state-side for more surgery and therapy. We have two new guys," Scout nodded, "I got an email."

"The new guys are trained the exact same, but they've served in Libya until getting transferred to us."

"Anything to know?" Scout raised an eyebrow; Kane knew he wanted to know if there were any quirks or problems reported from their former leaders.

"Both come highly recommended with no complaints," Kane shrugged.

"Why not rotate home with their platoon? Why come here?"

"Both are friends that come from a small town, but no one can answer that question," Kane watched Scout purse his lips, "I'll let you know if I find out why."

"Alright," Scout nodded, "Has the mail come?"

"Yes," Toby called from around the corner, "Although the delivery guy said it's ridiculous how loved we are considering we have the most mail he's ever seen coming out of a blackout."

"Are you coming in?" Scout asked standing with a frown coming around to see what Toby was doing.

"I think I'm going to need some help," Toby called standing at the door with quite a few canvas bags the size of large trash bags around his feet.

"What did he do dump it at the door with you and go, sir?" Kane grinned.

"Something like that," he nodded, "Help me would you, hey Mercer get over here!" He was looking outside having seen

Mercer walking across the street. He came over and looked at the bags, "What the heck?"

"Never mind get a few guys to come help too," Toby pointed to barracks.

"No, we can get it," Scout murmured, "Come on."

They grabbed a bag a piece and put it in Scout's office, turned and made three trips a piece. Scout sighed, "Alright let's divide and conquer."

They each took a bag and started sorting it. There were boxes in each one and Scout had them put each box against the wall. Once they had the boxes stacked the letters were merged together. Scout had everyone rounded up for mail and Mercer and Toby helped him take the boxes to the rec room. Scout noticed every person had a small box and he recognized his home address as the return address.

"We have angered the mail man," he announced, "I'm not sure what the pen pals were up to but I'm going to call names and you come up get your letters and Toby and Kane will find your box."

They all murmured softly after that for a moment as Kane and Toby started looking for names. Scout called each person and gave a stack of letters wondering why there were so many letters this blackout compared to the last one. Everyone was surprised to have at least two or three letters a piece. The box was light weight, and everyone frowned seeing the neat handwriting and wondering what it could be.

"Somebody just open the box already," Quinn said softly, "I'm dying to know what it is!"

Everyone laughed, and Scout looked to Gryffin who just got his box and letters, "Gryffin put Quinn out of his misery would you?"

Letters from Home

"Yes, sir," Gryffin opened the box and juggled the letters with it, "It's...it's a DVD, sir."

When everyone had their box and letters Scout saw Quinn stare blankly at his DVD, "Since you were so eager to know what it was how about you put the DVD in, so we can see it."

"Yes, sir," he nodded.

Adelina was at her desk, "Hey! So, you've been on blackout forever, but I've been busy. I'm about to show you just how amazing this is but first I'd like to say I had a lot of help. This is Letters from home 5 which is a personal video. I hope you enjoy!"

Adelina faded out and it turned to a video of interstate with an exit to Cave City and over to the driver, which was Skyelar who smiled, pointing forward which made the camera turn back to show they took the exit. They drove to a small house in town that had fence around it. The baying basset hound with the long ears came through. "Based on what Zaidee said we have the right house. I volunteer to dog sit anytime, Dude is so cute," Skye smiled.

An older man came onto the porch and frowned at the dog, "Dude shut it!"

Quinn laughed trying to hide the fact that he was fighting tears, "He's always barking."

"Sorry, he's always barking!" the older man shook his head, it fast forwarded through introductions and petting Dude who tried to lick the camera. It read across the top:

I told him to say hi not lick the camera :/

Adelina came back on at her desk, "So some of the families weren't tech-savvy so we travelled to record them. We asked everyone to answer one question. That question was if they

Letters from Home 147

could tell their Marine what they thought of them what would it be?

Quinton, Quinn's dad, came onto the screen again sitting in a love seat with his wife both dressed nice and Dude sitting next to Mrs. Bryant. "What would we say? We are so very proud of him. Quinn, you are everything we could have ever hoped for in a son. You are protecting people and serving your country, but we can't wait for you to come home," his father murmured.

"We love you, Quinn, and we miss you," Mrs. Bryant swiped her eyes.

"Well Debbie it's a video, don't cry," Quinton shook his head patting her hand.

"I can't help it; I haven't heard his voice in weeks! I miss his voice; I miss his mischievous eyes and that crooked smile when he thinks he could get away with anything."

"Quinn, you know your mom has cleaned this house spotless and if you don't call soon, I think she'll clean a hole in the stove or wear a hole in the floor from pacing."

"Quinton," she slapped his shoulder with a huffing laugh, "You know he's busy doing important work."

He smiled at the camera, "I've got bruises too, son, just call when you can. We love you and we miss you."

The basset hound bayed again and they all laughed. Adelina turned the camera to face her, "Dude says he misses your face too, I speak Bassett-ese."

"Because dogs speak different languages too?" Skye asked with a laugh.

"Yep," Adelina smiled. The movie fast forwarded showing they all stood and went out the door and to the car. They

Letters from Home

followed his parents to a local eatery and sat down and Adelina recorded a few seconds of the meal in front of her. "It's Quinn's favorite meal here with ice cream afterward," his mom murmured.

"Quinn, I'm trying it but as soon as you get home it's here for you!" Adelina murmured and suddenly it showed ice cream on a cone. They went to a few of his favorite places and then back to the house, "Sorry we have to leave so soon," Skye murmured to his parents, "This is a road trip to a few different states to meet other family members. It was so nice to meet you and don't hesitate to call me if you need anything."

"Thank you, sweetheart," his mom hugged both girls and she accepted a hug from Quinton too who looked at the camera, "I can't wait to hear his reaction to this. He knows we barely know how to work a cell phone, so this will be a massive surprise for Quinn."

"I'm sure he'll call as soon as he can and tell you all about it," Skye smiled, "Bye!"

They left, and it faded on the basset hound as it bayed again. Adelina came back on, "I know it's kind of short but it's of home. We wanted to give you a piece of home as soon as you got done on blackout because you'd be homesick and missing family. The pen pals all agreed not to video since it is home this time around. I hope we get them sent quickly enough, it's taken me longer than expected and any day you all will have the clear to call home. I hope you like it...this is your video master, Adelina Dale, Episode 5 complete. God bless and Semper Fidelis Marines."

Everyone was quiet as the video stopped and Quinn shook his head, "That damn dog never shuts up, but God, I miss him."

Kane touched his shoulder, "That was awesome dude."

Letters from Home

"Guess what," Quinn smiled looking in the small box again.

"What?" Hayes asked.

"I got a deck of cards," he held up tea mixes and the deck of cards.

Everyone had to share the TV, so everyone lounged and watched the DVDs. Everyone's started the same, Scout opened his letter and box, he didn't offer his to play yet but was surprised that Mercer asked to go next. Everyone hushed as it turned on.

Adelina spoke the same as Quinn's DVD and then it faded to a video that was obviously recorded by the family. It was Derek's sister and boys, "Hey Uncle Derek!"

"Hey Derek," his sister smiled, "We were told that this would be sent to you and to record a little of home for you and answer the question. So, the boys want to answer the question first. Boys?"

"Uncle Derek you are a superhero, I made you a picture," the youngest held up a picture of a crayon stick figure with a rifle protecting other stick figures. "You are the best-est uncle I have."

"And the coolest," the older boy grinned, "We can't wait for you to come home and see our new trampoline and jump on it with us. Maybe when you get home mom will give us a break from home school and we can stay up late, and you can teach us the con-constatasions-"

"Stars."

"-again."

"Alright boys," his sister laughed softly, "Go play so I can tell Uncle Derek how much I love him alright?"

Letters from Home

"That'll take forever," the youngest's shoulders sagged, "Mommy can't we call Uncle Derek?"

"Not yet sweetie, he's on blackout which means the telephones don't work yet," she smiled, "As soon as the phones work, he will call."

"Their phone company sucks," the oldest grumbled.

"Dylan Matthew!" she shook her head, "Go play with your brother."

"Fine," he sighed dragging the younger boy off screen.

"You aren't missing much other than the boys driving me crazy wanting to call you," she smiled, "I'm proud of you, I know it's a hard job and you have bad days especially the last few months, but I know you do your best and you are the best. I know it's my opinion and I don't know all the marines but Derek Mercer you are strong, you are courageous, and you serve your country. I couldn't be prouder and more honored being your sister. Half the stuff you do would send me into a terrified puddle on the floor. I honestly don't know how you do it. I love you more than you'd imagine and cannot wait for you to come home so I can hear your voice," she swiped at her cheek, "Yes, I'm lame enough to cry talking to a video, but I miss you. I hope they can edit the video because I am definitely not that tech savvy."

It blacked out and came back showing main street and after a few seconds it blacked out and went to a garden with a waterfall which played for a minute. Then it blacked out to show his parents who talked for a few minutes with the boys sitting with them.

"We love you Uncle Derek!" they called as the video faded back to Adelina.

Letters from Home

Mercer looked down at the letters he received and the picture the youngest had made. Kane noticed everyone had went except Scout, "Sir are you going to play yours?"

"I don't know if you all want to hear my family gush all over me," he shook his head.

"Hey, you listened to our family gush," Toby smiled, "Come on, sir."

"Fine," he handed the DVD over, "No laughing allowed."

They all chuckled, it was good for them to see that he was just like the rest of them. He sat forward wondering what would happen.

Adelina sat at the desk, "Hey Scout, I hope you are safe and sound, Skye has been super busy helping me and working a lot, but I managed to get her on video without duct tape you should be impressed with my mad skills! Hope you and the guys like this project I know it's definitely challenged me and made Skye step up for the families, they've been burning up her phone worried for you guys."

It faded out and came back to show Skye driving with the radio on low, "What would you say if Scout was here, Skye?"

"I'd say that even knowing from an early age that they were going to the marines, it never prepared me for this," she flashed a smile, "Are you recording me?"

"Yes, ma'am, it'd be unfair for everyone else to get a video and not him."

"Fine," she sighed, "So Scout we are driving to go see Quinn's family then Kane's family, and quite a few others over this week. I took vacation because I needed a break. It's different losing sleep because I stayed up talking to you and losing sleep from worrying. Blackouts are not my forte, so

Letters from Home 152

much happens in a single day with your guys that I wonder what's happened over a week, two weeks, now it's going on three weeks and I catch myself thinking just call already!"

It faded out, "This is Scout's favorite restaurant in town. Lately I can't come in here without crying because I miss him so much."

Skye laughed softly, "He laughed at the menu the first time we came in here, small towns have barbed wire fence all over the farmland do we really have to see it on a menu?"

She mocked a deeper voice and Adelina laughed softly, showing the menu, and then moving up to the wall of the marines not zooming in on the pictures but Scout saw the black gauze on Johnny's picture and it hit him again that his best friend was gone.

"What would you tell him? We've asked the same question all week, how would you answer it?"

"Everyone has said it all week, they are proud, and I feel the same, I am honored to be his cousin, he's served his country and yes, he picks my brain about what I think but he's one of the smartest people I know. I don't know how he does it but he's stronger than me for sure. I can deal with people I barely know and do surgeries all day long but to work in a high stress environment day in day out," she shook her head, "He is amazing. He cares about everyone on his team to the point of extreme. He cares if they are homesick if something is happening back home. I don't know how many times he's called me in middle of the night to talk, wanting me to check on somebody over here, to take care of things so his guys can focus. That's a true leader, I would follow him to hell and back but if there's a perfectly good plane he wants to jump out of, I'm out."

Letters from Home 153

Everyone laughed with her as it faded out with only Skye's voice breaking through, *"Scout I know it's been hard the last few months; your guys have had it rough this tour, I am praying for you guys and I hope this blackout is over soon. I love you and I hope you are safe."*

It showed her driving and singing Bon Jovi softly, Adelina was quiet as she recorded her singing different songs as she watched the road.

Adelina came back on again, *"This is supposed to be a family DVD, but I had someone ask to send you a small video as well."*

Johnny's entire family was there, *"We aren't sure if you will share this with everyone, but we hope you do. This is for them as well as you, Scout. We are proud of you boys and we are praying for you. This tour has been hard on all of you as well as us at home. Some may not know us, but we are the Miles family, Johnny was a scout sniper in your platoon. He loved all you guys and loved pranking you even more. We are the ones that sent the nerf guns and some other pranks for him to use. We hope this finds you all well and hope you all come home soon. If you need anything, please feel free to contact us. You were Johnny's family as well and family sticks together. Semper Fi and God Bless."*

Adelina came back on, *"Sorry it's short Scout, Skye misses you and didn't want to cry. You know she doesn't want you distracted so hides it well. She said to pass it along that she would have sent a video to the M&M but no name means she's at a loss on who to send it to so,"* she shrugged, *"Anyway on a different note please let me know what the guys thought of the video, I hope they look alright, I've been putting the videos together for three weeks and finished the vacation DVDs over the last three days and lack of sleep is making me wonder if I messed any of them up. I'd love a video from you guys if that's* *allowed. You should have a package coming soon as well. We are sending these on September 4th, the package will follow soon after, there are a few last-minute things to collect before sending it."*

Everyone sat quiet for a moment and Scout stood to get the DVD, "A good surprise, I think Adelina needs a visual confirmation that her efforts are not in vain. I will try to get my hands on a camera. Any questions for me?"

"Skye is your cousin?" Quinn asked surprised, "The one writing Mercer?"

"Yes," he met Quinn's eyes, "James shuffled the letters, so no one knew who wrote to whom."

He had confirmed James would continue the lie for their benefit, Quinn looked to Mercer, "Are you going to tell her who Mercer is?"

"That's Mercer's decision, we've talked about that already," Scout glanced around, "Other questions?"

"Are we going to have any more blackouts the remainder of our tour?" Kane asked.

"Not at this time, we are needed here, this is a trouble spot and they want their best here. Has everyone reached home?"

Everyone said yes sir although now they all wanted to call again to talk about their videos. Everyone held onto the DVDs like they were gold. Scout raised an eyebrow when Hayes made to talk and then stopped. "Hayes?"

"Any news on our boys that were injured?" he asked.

"They are going home and will be in physical therapy for a while. We have two new guys coming in tonight as their replacements," Scout glanced around, "Alright have a nice evening to yourselves."

They read letters and wrote back, chilling out for their day off, most shocked they had letters from many in their communities as well. Scout went to his office and set Skye's DVD in his desk to play again later. He missed her. He went to his meeting and asked if anyone had a video camera. Two other platoon commanders nodded that they had a guy that had a camera.

"What's this about?" his boss asked.

"My hometown has plenty of Marines in my platoon. They have been sending letters and videos to us. They have asked for a video back."

"What happened with all that mail earlier?" Jon asked, he was one of the platoon commanders, "The mail guy said that's the most mail he's ever seen coming out of blackout."

"My cousin is a pen pal with her friends. They sent individual DVDs and everyone's normal mail from home."

"That's a lot of mail," his boss was impressed, "How do you plan to record this video?"

"I plan to video quickly and send it with my two going home next week, just of the guys in the rec room and our home away from home. Nothing showing where we are in case something happens between delivery."

"Alright," he nodded, "How about we have Jon's guy record everyone and help you since he's an IT guy anyway?"

"Sure," Scout nodded as they went into serious business. When they finished and went to eat Scout looked at the time on his watch seeing it was almost nine at home. He called hearing exhaustion in her voice. "Did I wake you up?"

"No," she shook her head, "I just finished up and thought I missed your call. I am staying here for tonight in case they need help but I'm sleeping in our staff room."

"I see," he nodded, "The videos made it today and everyone has been watching them and coveting them like they are made of gold. Thank you for such an amazing gift, Skye. It meant a lot."

"I'm glad you got them today!" she smiled, "Quinn's basset hound was adorable, I may need to break down and get us a dog but I'm not home enough for one."

"Kane's talking of moving to our town," Scout laughed softly, "He could get the dog and you can dog sit to get your fix."

"Oh, good idea!" she laughed, "How are they?"

"We have two that were badly injured and headed home as soon as they are cleared to travel. Kane said they loved their DVDs and can't wait to be home."

"Adelina is about to die if she doesn't get feedback soon," Skye chuckled softly, "She loves sending videos to your guys but with that time crunch she is exhausted. Her great-aunt called me to come over and check on Adelina because she couldn't wake her up. I told Dina she was exhausted and would be fine in a couple days."

"Adelina mentioned another surprise?" Scout murmured.

"News travels fast in our small town. The pastor announced we were sending videos and planning to send a care package. The whole community dubbed Zaidee's coffee shop the drop point and she's barely got room for everything. We sent a care package to your platoon to share with your other platoons as well. Someone in the community decided you all needed a themed party so sent Hawaiian grass skirts, the flower

Letters from Home

necklaces, snacks, you name it and you got it coming. What did the mail man say?"

"The most mail he's ever seen for a platoon coming out of blackout and we must be loved."

"Well, be sure to invite everyone for the party there should be enough stuff to share."

"Yes ma'am," he chuckled, "I miss you, Skye, I can't wait to be home. I don't even mind the to-do list."

"I haven't started a to-do list yet," she stressed the yet in that sentence because there were things that needed fixed, but she hadn't mentioned them.

"I'll call you tomorrow night if I can," he could hear her fighting sleep and yawning.

"I'm sorry Scout," she shook her head, "Today was a difficult day, the only highlight was hearing your voice."

"Well, I'm glad you love my voice," he grinned.

"I wish I could hug you too but no such luck today," she smiled.

"How are your patients doc?" he asked seriously.

"I nearly lost three and had to call in the on-call doctor to come help out. Two are still in the woods but the rest are alright, broken bones mostly and monitoring them."

"Well, I'm glad, anyone I know?" he asked.

"No just passing through and we were the closest hospital. They are transferring to the big city tomorrow morning."

"Why?" he frowned.

"One lady said she didn't want her husband to die in a Podunk town like ours," Skye shrugged, "It actually will give me a break when they go. I don't mind them transferring but one doctor has already called me and congratulated me on saving them considering I found a heart murmur and nearly lost him. He said he would be sure to tell them as much as well."

"I'm glad you live in our Podunk town," he chuckled, "They need you there."

Chapter 8
Surprise Phone Call

"Hello?" Skye's voice was drowsy, he shouldn't have called, Scout would kill him for not getting permission first, "Scout? Are you alright?"

He didn't know what to say, she always wrote the things he needed to hear, the bible verses, the encouragement, he just wanted something to calm him down enough to sleep. He wasn't sleeping, he was tired—past tired—but being in enemy territory, getting attacked anywhere and at any time caused his inability to sleep. He tried to think of something but his mind was blank. Skye sighed, "God please wrap your arms around the boys over there. They need you so much. Give them wisdom, peace of mind, please give them rest. I don't know what's going on or if they are ok but protect them. You are the God of miracles, the God that can split the sea, show them you have them in your hands. In Jesus name, amen."

She heard a shaking breath on the other end of the line and said, "I wish I was there for you. I know I don't have the words to make it better, but a hug wouldn't hurt. Please say something you have me worried."

"Thank you."

The line went dead instantly, he left before anyone came into the phone room. She frowned it didn't sound like Scout but it was only two words so maybe it was and she wasn't sure. She frowned confused and wondered who it could have been if not Scout. It made her worry and the stress of not hearing from him made her sit heavily on the floor as stressed tears fell down her face. She was at the hospital break room, she prayed again for them and for her sanity, she couldn't lose Scout, and she was panicking.

Letters from Home

Skye slowly pulled herself together and continued to leave work and get home. It was the weekly get together with the girls to write and catch up and she needed to clean up the house and get ready. A half an hour later the phone rang again, and she answered instantly.

"Hello?" she asked worried.

"Skye," Scout's voice instantly told her that he was exhausted and upset.

"What happened?" she asked softly.

"I can't talk about it," he sighed, "It's not over yet but pray."

"Did you call a little bit ago?" she asked confused.

"No," his voice shone with confusion.

"Who called me?" she wondered looking out the window.

"What was said?" he asked wondering but thinking it wasn't possible.

"Nothing I thought it was you, nothing was said so I prayed and asked for you to talk to me that I was worried and whoever it was said thank you and hung up."

"I see," he sighed, "It's been bad, Skye. Could you pray again with me?"

She was shocked, he never brought up God or asked for prayer. She took a breather and prayed again asking for endurance, for peace of mind, for wisdom and confidence for Scout. For his men to get rest. Scout sighed as she finished and murmured, "Amen."

"Did you give anyone my number?" she asked confused.

"If it happens again pray and talk, Skye, if they got your number they need you," Scout sighed.

"Is it M&M?" she asked surprised.

"It could be anyone in the platoon, many families have your number and they could get it to the men. There is no security breach so don't worry, Skye."

"Alright," she nodded, "Is everyone alright?"

"A few cuts and bruises but no major injury. It must be your prayers protecting us, Skye because we shouldn't have come out without at least five dead."

"Is it a bad time to say I told you God listens to me?" she tried for funny and he gave a halfhearted chuckle.

"Over here is so challenging and you see so much, Skye, we can talk when I get home. Until then pray hard."

"You praying too? What do I pray for?" she asked worried as the girls started pulling in.

"Pray for strength, for smart decisions, for our protection of body and sound minds, everything you can think of," he sighed.

"Did you get mail since the DVDs?"

"We haven't been in since then," he sighed, "Who was it addressed to?"

"You," she sighed.

He glanced at the door to find Mercer standing there, dark shadows under his eyes. He had a difficult job the last few days as sniper he had lain in the heat watching over them for a full two days providing cover fire when needed and it took a ton out of him. "Skye, I have a meeting, I'll call you soon alright?"

"Love you," she whispered.

Letters from Home

"I love you too," he hung up.

Skye heard the knock on the door and called for them to come in, Alara met her gaze as Adelina sat on the bar stool, "What's wrong, Skye?"

"Scout just called, he said they have been out the past two days and it is bad, a miracle they didn't have any fatalities from the sounds of things. I just…it was weird; I had a phone call before that before I left the hospital. It was from someone in his platoon that never spoke. Scout said if they called me that there was a reason and to just talk or pray whatever to help them."

"Do you think it was M&M?" Adelina asked as Rashel and Nadira came in.

"I don't know he thanked me and hung up. I thought it was Scout but then he called. I'm worried about them. He said it's not good."

"Did they get the care packages?" Rashel asked.

"They haven't had mail since the DVDs because they've been on a mission."

"Wow, that was two days ago," Adelina looked surprised.

"Yeah," Skye nodded, "Let's write and watch a movie or something."

"Alright," they agreed. Skye needed distracted and they were fine with helping her become distracted.

Scout hung up from talking to Skye, he knew she was confused and worried but if it was any of his unit, he wasn't going to hold it against them. Skye always seemed to instill in others a sense of peace that very few people possessed. Mercer stood at attention in the doorway waiting for Scout to invite him in.

"Come in, Derek," Scout rubbed his eyes, feeling his hands trembling so folded them on his desk tightly.

"Sir," Mercer came in and sat across from him.

"You hydrated?" Scout noticed his lip was busted and skin looked burnt from the desert.

"They released me with a clean bill of health, sir," he agreed.

"You are a life saver, I'm glad you are okay," Scout sighed, relieved.

"It was only two days, sir," Derek rubbed his head, feeling the tingle of sunburn when he touched the back of his neck.

"Two days of no rest and little to no food or water in 120-degree weather," Scout shook his head, "What can I do for you?"

"I was to inform you I am cleared for duty," he murmured.

"Get some sleep, Derek," Scout patted his shoulder, "Hopefully we won't be on duty for a few days."

"Yes, sir," Derek nodded standing.

"I know I can't fall asleep," Scout told him honestly, "Last week done me in."

He was referring to the attack on their base, the enemy combatants blew a hole in the wall and tried their best to kill all the Marines on site. It was just before midnight; most the camp was asleep and being woke to gunfire and explosions sent a man into sleepless nights after such events. Derek was

Letters from Home 164

surprised Scout admitted it but nodded, "I used to laugh when my nephew said he was afraid to close his eyes because the monsters might get him...I think I owe him an apology when he's older and wouldn't freak out if I told him there really were monsters out to get me."

"Security is up, get as much rest as you can, I take naps during the day to catch more sleep," Scout knew the red rimmed eyes weren't from lack of sleep but from keeping his eyes open for so long in the desert when he was keeping them alive. Sand irritation was something that drove them all a little mad because their eyes weren't used to it even after so many months out here.

"I miss home," Derek sighed, "The woods, that pond at your house, I'll bypass the city but take the family and friends."

"Believe me, we get home and I'm all about having you all over any time you need," Scout smirked, "Getting sunburns from fishing and playing around instead of this."

"Sounds good sir," Derek stood and shook his hand, "Good night."

"Night Mercer," Scout watched him leave.

Four days later, very few calls from Scout, and no more quiet phone calls from the mystery caller, and a young man in uniform came to Skye's door. She froze seeing him, "Scout?" she asked knowing how they informed loved ones of a death but not sure what it meant for just one man to arrive. The man looked surprised and concerned; Skye paled instantly and searched his eyes. He wasn't in dress blues or with a chaplain so he wasn't sure why she had panicked.

"Ma'am, your cousin is fine, I'm sorry to scare you!" he played with his hat for a moment before becoming still again, "I was asked to deliver a package personally to Skyelar Hamilton. One of the Marines at the VA knew I was getting released and headed passed this town."

"Oh," Skye sagged in relief, "I've heard there has been some trouble in their area and I haven't talked to him in the last few days. What is the package?"

"This ma'am," he handed her a small box, "Jameson said it was important."

"It's late are you driving through?" Skye asked. She didn't recognize the name but that didn't mean anything, knowing Scout it was probably him that sent it.

"I'm stopping for the night before continuing in the morning," he nodded.

"There's an inn just outside of town," she met his gaze, "I'll call them and get a room for you. Come in, please."

He stepped in and glanced around, "Thank you ma'am but I can take care of it."

"No, it's my pleasure," she shook her head, "Have you ate supper?"

"No ma'am," he frowned.

"Good," she grabbed her cell phone and called Rashel, "Call the girls and come over now."

"What's wrong?"

"Surprise," she hung up and called pizza to be delivered. Adelina beat everyone there coming in and pointing to the door. She heard voices, a low voice talking about physical therapy and Skye asking questions.

"Skye whose car?" she asked before coming around the corner.

"It's David Bass' he's a Marine heading home from the VA hospital."

"Was he in the platoon?" Adelina asked, surprised to find the Marine sitting at the table with her.

"No but Jameson was, and they are friends," Skye held up the box she hadn't opened.

"What's that?" Adelina stepped closer.

"Nothing until the others get here," she shook her head, "I haven't opened it."

"Oh," she sagged, calling Serabeth, "Hurry up!"

"You try getting a 3-year-old in the car when it's time for bed," Serabeth snapped driving fast, "I'm at the driveway waiting on Nadira to hurry up and turn."

Adelina opened the door and David looked surprised, "Ms. Hamilton?" David asked finding more cars surrounding his car.

"We are pen pals with Scout's platoon," Adelina explained, "We have sent videos, letters, the works."

"I bet they love that," he flashed a smile, "Our group barely got mail."

The pizza was right behind Zaidee who looked like she just woke up, "What's this about?"

"Thanks Gordon," Skye paid for the pizza and brought it in, "We've got mail."

"Hand delivered," Adelina added nodding to David who looked at all the curious girls surrounding him. He met each,

Letters from Home

shaking hands, and looked at the small box a little bigger than a sheet of paper and about an inch thick. They all grabbed drinks and Adelina seemed to bounce impatiently to the point that all of them noticed she was itching to tear into it.

"Open it, Skye," Nadira smiled.

"Adelina gets to open it," Skye shook her head, "Come on."

Adelina tore into it to find letters and DVDs, "They sent videos back!"

"Come on, let's get food and watch the videos," Skye smiled grabbing paper plates and the pizza sitting it on the coffee table. She thanked Nadira for grabbing napkins and they all sat watching the DVD labeled #1.

"Hey Adelina, I'm Roger, I'm in a different platoon but was asked to video for Commander Scout's group so everyone could be recorded. I hope you enjoy my efforts it was quick and not as professional as yours that Commander Scout showed me since I don't have the technology to play with here. Hope you enjoy!"

"Finally!" Adelina squealed, Princess Evie giggled at her and Skye nearly spit her drink as she laughed.

Suddenly it went to a party with grass skirts and coconut bras, leis, and loud music. Scout was nowhere to be seen but a few guys yelled and the music cut. "Adelina your videos are amazing, you ladies are wonderful, and we appreciate you guys so much. As you can see, we got a special delivery from the Boss. All the platoons are having separate parties since we are all on a schedule. This is our platoon party now. My name is Zane Wolf, beside me is Quinn Bryant, Kevin Hayes, and Brian Murphy. You will have to find the other pen pals later. Thanks again ladies, this is an amazing party, you should add party planning to your resumes for real!"

Letters from Home

"I hope they got all the pen pals," Nadira murmured.

"I want to see Gryffin, a face with a name is so much easier!" Alara agreed.

Roger took off walking again and found some guys chilling out in the corner playing cards and relaxing. Roger knew who the pen pals were, so he paused and said, "Video for Adelina say hey!"

The card game stopped, and Kane stood up, "I'm Kane McCullough, thanks ladies, the new cards are much appreciated!"

Roger saw a nerf ball get tossed and caught sight of Derek although Scout gave him instructions not to mention pen pals as he recorded. Derek paused catching the nerf ball and watching Roger and then continued tossing the nerf ball after a slight wave of hello.

"Some people just don't know how to party," Roger sighed, "Maybe they can't dance."

"I heard that," Derek yelled over the music.

"Good!" Roger yelled back, and the camera caught the nerf ball flying at him and Roger catching it right before it could hit the lens.

Derek sat up and Skye noticed a cut on his cheek, "Come on dude give it back."

"Come and enjoy the party bro," Roger offered.

"I am," *he held up his hand and Roger tossed it back and turned to continue. He stopped seeing Gryffin with a coconut bra on,* "Oh boy."

"Hey ladies!" Gryffin grinned, "Dance with me!"

Letters from Home

Roger kept the camera steady and on Gryffin who shimmied and laughed, "I'm Gryffin! Hey, you should come with me to the Rocky Mountains and rock climb with me when we get home! The rock wall was a decent job a few more times visiting there, and you can climb the mountain no problem."

"Hey!" Scout appeared as if out of nowhere and caught Gryffin's shoulder and the music cut as everyone came to attention. Scout smiled, "As you were! Gryffin if you endanger my girls, you will have some trouble on your hands."

"Yes, sir!" Kane grinned from behind them. It was a dangerous smile and Scout fought a smile, "How are we enjoying the party gentlemen?"

Everyone cheered, and his eyes landed on the camera, "You girls have went above and beyond for us and we thank you from the bottom of our hearts!"

Roger came back on and smiled, "The party was so loud that they broke a speaker on the radio. Like I said before I hope you enjoy these videos. Adelina it's all I've heard from the guys is how amazing you are to have made everyone a DVD."

Skye changed the DVDs and hit play. *Kane was there, "Nadira thank you for writing to me and for the videos, it's helped so much the past few months."*

The video played with a few guys that weren't pen pals on each DVD as well as their pen pals talking. The last DVD was put in and Roger appeared. Bass sat watching, seeing the sincerity in each face on camera and the rapt attention the girls sat in, pizza forgotten as they played each one. He wondered what the story was with these guys but said nothing as the next video played.

Letters from Home

"This is for Skye mostly, I was told not to share who the pen pal was until he was ready, but a lot of others want to talk to you."

Kane came on first, "I know you are expecting your cousin, but Skye I have to say you are amazing and don't quit on M&M. He needs you more than you know. I also want to make sure you are part of the VA because to be honest I don't think I will ever let another doctor see me except for you. You are amazing, and I think we can all agree to trust you girls explicitly."

"Hey Skye," Quinn was there, "Dude really liked you. I will have to make a trip to visit you girls and meet in person. You are all a breath of fresh air around here. Keep the videos and letters coming they are amazing and a blessing."

"Hey cousin!" Scout appeared, "Evidently, I'm low man on the totem pole. Everyone wants to talk to you. I had to pull rank to get to record this! Tell Adelina she doesn't need approval for those DVDs she could make dirt look good on her camera. When we passed out the DVDs everyone held them like they were gold around here. No one expected much mail or for a personalized DVD, but everyone was hiding tears as they watched the DVDs. The dog…Dude…got all of us teary eyed like mushy girls around here. I miss you, Skye, and I can't wait to get a bear hug when I get home. From the look of things, we won't be able to video again after this since Roger's platoon is headed home. We are scheduled for a month and a half more, but you know it always changes. I hope you are alright the last couple days have been rough, so I am hoping the inconsistency isn't stressing you out. Tell the girls to keep writing. I will tell you if anything changes for now be prepared for some rough couple days more. All I can say is it's getting more dangerous over here but so far everyone is alright. I love you, Skyelar Hamilton."

Skye noticed the window had been bright to the side as the others all talked, Scout was the only one that it was black outside. He had waited for everyone to go before recording. She sat back and tensed as Roger came on screen again.

"One more special request to speak to you, Ms. Hamilton."

"Hello Ms. Hamilton, you don't know me but I'm Scout's boss. Over all the platoons his men are doing better with dealing with the stress of being away from home and it's mainly because of you and your friends. Thank you for that, they are one of the best platoons I have, and I need them focused, keep praying and encouraging them. God bless you ladies!"

Skye sighed, "It feels like forever since I've seen his face, he's lost weight."

"Did we get letters too?" Laikynn asked yawning.

"Yeah," Skye passed out the letters and the girls left with their personal DVDs. They all felt relieved and excited to have gotten DVDs back and letters from their pen pals. Adelina was deliriously happy and couldn't quit smiling. Laikynn thought it was funny all the guys brought up her arm being shoved up the cow and thinking it was hilarious. Skye looked up to David offered a room but he shook his head, "I don't want to wake you when I wake early in the morning ma'am. Thank you for letting me watch this and meet you amazing ladies!"

Skye smiled and called Morgan, an older lady that owned the inn, "Hey Morgan, how are you?"

"Good Skye," she smiled, "How are you?"

"Good, I have a Marine standing in front of me needing a place to crash for the night. You have a room?"

"Of course," Morgan nodded, "Scout's man?"

"No just passing through and delivering a package," Skye smiled, "His name is David Bass, I'm sending him your way."

"Alright," she agreed, and David left to go that way. Skye called Morgan back and told her to send her the bill for the room and Morgan agreed surprised. Skye went to bed soon after.

In middle of the night, she woke to her phone ringing, "Hello?"

Nothing.

"I hope you are alright with me praying because I don't know what else to do from here," she rubbed her eyes, "I don't know what to say to make it better. God thank you for another day, for giving us the courage to face it, please help this Marine…whoever it is God you know his heart and you know what he needs. Answer his heart's cry, give him peace, calm him, steady him, carry him when he doesn't think he can do it by himself. Let him feel the support, the warmth of your love, I pray that whatever is happening that it settles down and the rest of the tour is a cakewalk for him. God bless him, comfort him, and surround him with love. In Jesus name, amen."

"Amen," he said softly.

"Can I have a name?" she asked feeling tired.

"You can call me M&M," he seemed to hesitate surprised he answered her.

"I'd love a real name," she smiled slightly.

"C-could you tell me what it was like growing up with Scout and J—…sorry forget it. Sorry for waking you up, Skyelar."

"No don't go," she sat up, "Were you close to Johnny there?"

"Yeah," he cleared his throat.

Letters from Home

"What do you want to know?" she asked frowning.

"How are you so positive?" he sat in the empty room filled with phones. Everyone else was at chow, he sat in the far corner head down on the table.

"I...I pray a lot; I have bad days but ultimately Johnny wouldn't want me to pout around for him. He would kick my butt if I cried for him. He said he didn't want people to cry for him, he wanted people to party it up because he would be in a better place, to remember the good times and remember him as the goof he was." Skye ignored the tears leaking from the corners of her eyes slipping to her hair as she laid in bed with her eyes closed. She never imagined talking to someone in the platoon about Johnny.

"He was a goof," Derek murmured, "I feel like it was my fault he's gone."

"No," Skye's voice took a tone of authority he hadn't heard before, "Johnny knew what he signed up for, he knew things can go sideways fast and no one is at fault for when it happens. He'd kick your butt for blaming yourself. Don't beat yourself up for something out of your control."

"Can you tell me stories of him in your letters?" he asked softly, "I have a tough time remembering the good times when I saw his death."

Mercer fought to keep his voice steady, he was exhausted from all the missions and lately all he could remember of Johnny was him getting hit. Mercer knew there were other memories but that was what he saw when he closed his eyes.

"You know he's the reason I write letters all the time?" Skye asked softly fighting to stay calm, cool, and collected. She couldn't break down; M&M needed her and she didn't want to let anyone down.

"Really? How's that?"

"He was helping us clean out the attic with grandpa and he found a box of letters. Grandpa explained that grandma wrote him while he served overseas and him and Scout made me swear to write to them when they went to the Marines. Even when I was barely in school, they already had plans to go to the Marines. Back then they had this superhero ideology of their career. Johnny told Scout once he was going to be a sniper and marry me," Skye laughed softly, "He was always like a brother and we went on one date and realized it never would work out, we ended up cutting the date off before we even ate dinner and went to find Scout and go to the shooting range."

"Johnny swore he'd be single forever," Derek smirked, "Said he was too much for one girl to handle."

"Of course, he did," Skye laughed softly, "Truth be told he didn't think he could handle the married life."

"Most of us would rather go to war than face that option," Derek murmured.

"You sound like it would be more dangerous to marry," she cocked her head waiting.

"It's easier, I think," Derek shrugged. He had a front row seat to his sister's short marriage and the crazy life before they divorced, the struggle his sister had with raising the kids alone with no support.

"Are you married?" Skye smirked.

"No, I came close to being engaged when I was fresh out of high school but…some girls like to break a guy's heart."

"Not all girls are diabolical," she promised, "For real M&M are you going to write this girl back?"

"I don't want to depress you," he studied his shoes not noticing anyone at the door.

"It's hard to do," she murmured, "I have seen a lot and suffered a lot, M&M. I'm sure a letter won't hurt me. I'd like to hear some stories of Johnny from someone that was close to him and maybe your real name sometime soon?"

"Maybe, get some sleep. Thanks for the talk," he murmured.

"Anytime," she sighed, "I'm praying for you."

"I need it," he hung up and turned finding Scout standing there. Mercer stood at attention, "Have a seat, Derek."

"Sir," he sat and studied the desk in front of him, his eyes red rimmed. Scout sat food in front of him, "You need to eat, Derek."

"Sir...I talked to my sister the other day and she had called Skye before the blackout ended to try and find out when it would be over. I asked for Skye's number," Derek looked to Scout to see if he was upset.

"Okay," Scout nodded.

"I wanted to get permission to call her, but you were in a meeting when I tried to ask before," he looked at his hands.

"You called her already," Scout nodded slightly, "It's fine Derek. She's your pen pal and if you want to talk to her then that's fine."

"You knew I called?" Derek asked surprised.

"She had a mysterious blocked call, she thought it was me, but you have a reputation for not communicating so I put two and two together a few days ago."

"Does she know?" Derek asked still not sure he wanted her to know who he was.

"No, I told her to talk if no one speaks on the phone. She was concerned there was a security problem."

"She's so much calmer than my family, I don't want my sister or parents to worry and when I went to call them, I ended up calling her. She prayed, and I guess it helped me calm down enough to get through a phone call to everyone the first time around."

"I'm glad," Scout nodded, "Get some rest, we may be called on again soon and I want you to have some time to be relaxed."

"Are you sure you are cool with me calling her?" Derek stood knowing Scout had other things to do before he could relax.

"Derek," Scout stood and stepped around to the chair, "If someone can help you relax enough to get some decent rest after the hell we just faced out there, then call them. If it's Skye if it's your mom, whoever it is I don't care."

Mercer had laid a few days in a hide covering them when the enemy surprised them in a valley to the north of their camp. He slipped to higher ground without the enemy seeing him and then covered them until the other platoons came to help them out. He saved more than Scout would like to admit, including himself, and if Skye could help the guy sleep without being so exhausted as to pass out, then so be it.

"Thank you, sir," Derek took the food and headed out of the call area. Scout waited until Derek was gone before calling Skye.

"Scout?" she asked instantly.

"He talked to you," Scout was amazed.

"Still won't tell me his name," she sighed, "Is he alright? He asked about Johnny and asked me to write about growing up with him."

"He's going through a rough time, Skye."

"Alright," she nodded, "Night Scout, I love you."

"Love you," he hung up and went back to work.

Chapter 9
Trouble

Skye drove home from another late shift and frowned seeing a car parked in the driveway. She got out of the car and saw a man in military uniform, it had been days since hearing from Scout or M&M, she had written plenty of letters along with the girls, all of them putting a letter almost every day of encouragement and funny stories. Skye always worried when she saw a Marine standing at her door when it had been a few days. She met his gaze, "Hello."

"Ma'am," he stood at parade rest near the door to the house.

"Can I help you?" she asked confused.

"I'm Jameson, I was part of the platoon with Commander Chase."

"Oh, you were injured a few weeks ago. How are you doing?" she asked still confused at what he was doing at her doorstep.

"I'm good, I'm doing physical therapy and transferred to the VA closer to my house in Texas. I stopped here to let you know that I heard from Commander Chase and it looks as if they will be gone longer than they thought."

"I see," she nodded, "Thank you for the information. There was another Marine injured in your platoon, what was his name?"

"Williams, ma'am," he paused for a moment, "I just wanted to thank you for your encouragement for um…you call him M&M. He's saved all of us at least once if not twice and he has been a little out of sorts the last six months and it's good to see a spark of the old humor we all miss."

"How long have you been here, Jameson?" she asked going in and setting her stuff down.

Letters from Home

"A half hour, ma'am, not long."

"My schedule is crazy, I'm sorry," her phone rang, and she glanced down to see the hospital calling she gave an apology again and took the call, "This is Doctor Hamilton."

"Hey Skye," Alara murmured, "We have a problem, any chance you can come back in?"

"Depends on the problem to if I want to," she sighed, "What is it now?"

"We have a transfer request from the VA for a Marine last name Williams, you are the only doctor here that is part of the VA, they have designated the office next door as the VA office. Walsh said he was trying to get the information on what needed to happen to be able to do surgeries so our Marines in town wouldn't need to go to a different hospital out of town for anything."

"So why do I need to come in?" Skye asked confused.

"You need to sign the request and provide your VA information," Alara didn't get frustrated knowing Skye was in before her and had worked through lunch and hadn't ate supper yet.

"It can't wait for tomorrow?" Skye asked plaintively but Alara sighed.

"Do you have a scanner at the house?" Alara asked.

"Yes," she nodded, "I have a printer and scanner."

"I'm emailing them," Alara told her to have a good night and hung up.

"Sorry Jameson are you stopping somewhere or driving straight through?"

Letters from Home

"I'm driving straight through, I just wanted to thank you."

"It's my pleasure," she smiled, "If you need anything let me know."

"Thank you, ma'am," he nodded and limped toward the stairs, "Have a nice night."

"Have you had supper?" she asked, "I can make something before you go."

"I've already had an early supper at the coffee shop in town."

"Zaidee took care of you then," she smiled.

"I met most the girls except Alara, the others said she was working but I met most of you. I best be getting on the road."

"If you would let me know when you get home, so I know you made it alright?" Skye knew it was absurd, but she worried about people driving at night and fresh from overseas she just wanted to make sure he was alright.

"Yes, ma'am," he flashed a smile, "Have a good night."

"Thank you, drive safe, Jameson."

He left, and she went to the computer to do what Alara had asked. She scanned the signed copy back to her and went to bed, not wanting food, too stressed and tired to eat. The phone rang at one in the morning, she groaned before answering it. "Hello?"

"Skye listen," Scout's voice was urgent, and she sat straight up.

"What's wrong, Scout?"

"I've got three men wounded. They are critical, our field hospital is only so good. They patched them up and sent them to the VA hospital at Nashville probably about seven or eight

Letters from Home 181

hours ago. Kane was injured, he's refusing every doctor but you. I told him I'd call you. The other two are going to the same hospital. It's Charlie Sweet and Gordon Ramey, I don't know if the MCHQ has contacted them."

"Scout how are you?" she asked seriously.

"I'm exhausted, Skye, our platoon is showing how exhausted we all are. I haven't slept in three days and my hands keep shaking when I'm in camp," he sighed frustrated, "Look Skye I've got ten other men injured and I don't have time to talk, if the family has questions, they will probably call you. HQ will notify them that they were injured."

They had been out too much and not enough time between. The territory they were covering was still too turbulent to do much more than go out and get attacked by anyone. He saw so much that should have killed him and his men.

"I've got it, when will they land?"

"They left a few hours ago. We were still coming back in when they were sent your way. This is the first few minutes I've had to call you."

"Listen to me, Scout," Skye had written what he said down quickly and was hearing his terse voice, "When you get time to sleep, I want you to eat before you sleep. You are shaking because your body is exhausted, and your sugar is probably low. Were you hurt?"

"Bruises and scrapes but nothing else," he shook his head looking up to see Toby standing there.

"I'm praying, Scout, be careful," she murmured, and he rubbed his eyes.

"Thanks, Skye, I love you."

"I love you more," she heard the phone call end and bowed her head. She called Nadira, "Call Martha and the boys. I want to know they are aware and headed this way."

"What's wrong?" she was instantly awake.

"Kane was hurt and is heading to Nashville. He's refusing any other doctor, so I'm headed that way."

"I'll call them and be at your house in a moment," Nadira murmured hanging up instantly.

Skye received two calls and both asking how bad it was, but Skye was honest that it was a quick call from her cousin and she didn't have all the details. She told Mrs. Sweet, Charlie's mom from the other side of town, Skye would drive them if they hadn't coordinated with HQ for provided travel, her husband just had surgery and wasn't allowed to drive, and Mrs. Sweet was too emotional to drive. The Sweet family had coordinated with HQ. Ramey family lived in another town and stated they coordinated as well. Skye pulled the backpack from under her bed, packed with some clothes and essentials, and got ready. Nadira was at her door soon enough. Skye text Alara that she was heading to Nashville for an emergency and Alara text back that she would let the other doctors know she was taking off for an emergency and Skye called the VA hospital.

"We were trying to find your contact information, but you are so new that your information hasn't hit the database yet."

"I'm headed there now, I live two hours away," Skye murmured, "The families have been notified and I haven't been to your hospital, so I would like to have the patient information and any information I need sent to my email."

"I usually take these cases but will be in with the other two Marines coming in. Dr. Porter will be there to meet you and answer any questions you may have, and he can assist you if you need."

"I will decide when I see his file. Can you tell me what I'm walking into?" she asked.

"The information is sketchy at best," he sighed, "The file says he's got internal bleeding, if he makes it to us, it's a race against time to save him."

"Where is the wound?" Skye asked frowning confused why there wasn't much information.

"Stomach and the bleeding was slowed but they couldn't see where it was still bleeding from and decided to send him over and he is awake enough to demand you and Tennessee."

"All three are from Kentucky and Tennessee, I will be there as quickly as possible."

Skye glanced at Nadira and saw she was fighting tears knowing that was just one of the boys and wondering how bad he was, she knew the family now and prayed silently. Skye called Scout, "Hello?"

"Scout, hey I have Nadira with me and we are headed to the hospital. From the sounds of it the file is slim on what I'm walking into for Martha's husband. Can you give me more information?"

"I can tell you that we walked into hell and a wall blew up and it had rebar. I saw pieces imbedded in their skin, but I don't know how bad it is Skye."

"Are you alright?" she asked, "How's everyone else?"

"Zane and Gryffin have some injuries and a couple broken fingers but fine. The ten were all said to be fine. Everyone here is worried about our Dad, Skye."

Letters from Home

"You tell them that I'm on my way and doctor's orders are for them to rest and let me do the worrying alright?"

"We should have the next two days off to recover," Scout murmured.

"I'll call you with news when I get some," she nodded, "Get some sleep between now and then, it isn't a request, Commander Chase."

"Yes, ma'am," he sighed, and she hung up. She glanced at Nadira as she drove quickly, seeing the unshed tears and knowing they all were worried. She caught her hand and squeezed it, "He's a fighter, he'll be good in a few days."

"Thank you, Skye," she sighed.

They arrived at the hospital before the boys were due to show up. She led to the waiting area and gave her keys to Nadira in case she wanted to go get something to eat. She followed the doctor to the back and was introduced to the on-call nurses and read through the file of his history and prepared for surgery.

A few hours later she found the café and ate something quickly as she read, it was morning and she had missed the breakfast traffic luckily. Nadira had text her that Martha was there. She heard the nurses saying a helicopter landed and to be ready. She washed up and prepared for a long few hours, praying for steady hands and guidance along with Scout's team to get rest and continued to pray as the nurses did the routine of confirming the patient and information about him. She studied him, finding the nurses were quiet until she started asking for things.

Seven hours later they finished with Kane. She stepped out to find Martha and the boys there, she was exhausted and looked terrible with no makeup on, but Martha wouldn't care. She

Letters from Home

looked at Martha and the boys as she stepped into the waiting room, Lane caught sight of her first, "How's dad, Skye?"

"He's tough," she nodded, "He's sleeping and will be in ICU for a while to see how it goes. I'll know more when he wakes up."

"What about our boys?" Mr. Sweet asked.

"I just got out of surgery, has the doctor not come out yet?" she asked.

"No," Mrs. Sweet started to cry.

"Mrs. Sweet it isn't uncommon for the surgery to take a long time. Let me go check on them and see if I can get an answer."

"Thank you, Skye," Martha swiped her eyes.

"It's not me," Skye murmured pointing up, "Keep praying."

The doctors were still working and amazed that Skye was finished already. They invited her to help each of them and they all finished quickly. Skye found the families to tell them the surgeries went well, and they were in ICU. The other two doctors took over the conversation as she went to find Kane in ICU. Nadira sat with one of the boys helping with summer school work. She had called in as well. Dr. Walsh had told her to take the time they needed to make sure the boys were alright to get them home. Something Skye loved about the small community and hospital was that everyone pulled together to cover for each other when things went sideways.

Skye tapped at the door and came in to check his machines and looked at Martha, "It's going to be alright, Martha."

"I just need to hear his voice," she whispered.

Skye hugged her hard and closed her eyes, "I know."

Letters from Home

A nurse interrupted her with updated CT scans and an MRI to look at for Kane and she stepped out to look over it. She sighed relieved, "Thank you, Lord."

No internal bleeding was found on the brain or anywhere else. She had gotten all the issues taken care of and she hoped he'd wake soon. She went back in and set the CT on the backlight to show Martha, "It looks good, Martha, it's just a matter of time for him to wake. He's on Morphine and that may be what is taking him so long to wake up. He's exhausted and been through a lot."

"Visiting hours are almost over," Martha murmured aware they kept strict rules. Lane already came in with Ezekiel so they all had saw him and Martha now needed to figure out where they were going to stay for the night.

"Nadira got two rooms for us all to stay close by," Skye murmured reading the text message that Adelina had called around for a cheap place and after explaining she got everyone a room for a full week to stay with family free of charge.

"She didn't have to do that," Martha instantly teared up and Skye touched her shoulder. They saw that Adelina had been up at 3am the night they were all driving, to get the rooms for them.

"Martha it's alright the hotel close by has heard about the incident and insisted that we go there and let them take care of you."

Martha's hand was around Kane's, it was bandaged but she wasn't anywhere near the bandages, "I haven't ever seen him this hurt, Skye."

"He will recover, and this will be a bad memory," Skye promised.

Martha sighed, "I hope he wakes up soon."

Letters from Home 187

"Do we have to leave him here?" Lane asked, and Martha gasped.

"He just tightened his fingers," she searched his face and noticed his eye that wasn't swollen was cracked barely open, "Hey Babe!"

He started to cough with the tube down his throat. Skye went around and touched his cheek, "Kane, hold on and try to relax."

He tried to stop gagging and she wrapped a glove around the tube and pulled it out. He winced and rasped, "Thank you, Skye."

"Anything for you," Skye smiled and told Martha, "Don't stay too long, I'll be back in a moment to check on him."

"Sweet and Ramey?" Kane looked worried.

"They haven't woken up yet, but surgery went well," she smiled, "I'll be back in a bit, you have a bunch of worried Marines over there waiting on me to tell them you are alright."

"Tell them you fixed me up good," he tried to grin, but his face was too swollen and bruised to do that.

"Don't worry I got you," she smiled and walked outside. She looked at the nurse, "I know it's against the rules but he's awake and his other two boys will want to see him while he's up."

"You're the doctor," the head nurse smiled, and she walked out and got Nadira's attention, all three came in and Kane tried to smile but couldn't. Nadira checked his monitors and then met his gaze.

"Nice to finally meet you but you better not think I'm happy it's under these conditions young man," she greeted.

Letters from Home

"Don't make me laugh," he winced as he tried not to laugh. Case smiled as Martha turned to Nadira, "What time is it?"

"Almost that time," Nadira winced, "Boys, as a nurse I know you want to stay with dad, but he needs his rest. Let's give mom a moment and see if the Ramey family is going to the hotel or getting something to eat first."

"Is Skye coming with us?" Ezekiel froze at the door holding everyone up as he looked up at Nadira worried.

"I think so," she frowned, "What's wrong?"

"Skye has to take care of dad!" he wailed.

"Oh, sweetie it's okay!" Nadira tussled his hair, "Skye knows if she needs to stay or if Kane's going to be fine for a night."

"What's wrong in here?" Skye asked appearing at the door confused.

"Are you staying to make sure dad's okay?" Ezekiel asked tears running down his face.

"I can't if you are going to cry," she raised an eyebrow, "Otherwise I have to make sure you don't get the endless-tears syndrome."

He was eight and wasn't about to fall for it, "That's not a thing."

"I'm a doctor, I had a little boy, ten years old, couldn't quit crying, it lasted seven days it was horrible," she smiled, "I planned on staying with Kane but if you start that then I have to make sure you don't cry yourself into a puddle."

"I won't cry," he swiped desperately at his eyes and looked back at Kane, "Bye dad."

"Love you," Kane was fighting sleep already.

Skye went to call Scout, hearing his voice alert and sounding one hundred percent better, "Chase."

"You slept at least," she sighed.

"More like completely crashed for ten hours. What happened to calling me when you were out of surgery."

"I got out of surgery about an hour ago and was checking on Kane before I called you," she sighed, "Kane is awake and talking to family."

"He's good then?" Scout asked.

"As long as he doesn't get an infection and his oxygen levels stay up. He's got some cracked ribs and it wasn't pretty. It took seven hours for me to put humpty back together again. The other two are still asleep the other doctors let me help them with finishing up. All the families are here and I'm staying the night just in case they need me."

"The families are staying at the hospital?" he frowned.

"No," Skye shook her head, "I am staying, they are going to a hotel which is paid for the week."

"Really? Who paid?" he frowned.

"Well Adelina called around to find us all a room and explained the situation and a hotel manager insisted that we go there and stay for the week," Skye shrugged.

"You aren't going tonight?" Scout asked.

"No, I want to make sure the guys are safe before I rest," she shook her head again, "Get more sleep for me. I want to know I don't have to worry about you too."

"Alright, I'll let the guys know the update," he sighed, "Are you sure?"

"Yeah," she nodded, "I love you."

"Love you too," he smirked as she hung up.

Skye knew it would be a sleepless night and told the night staff that she was going to the chapel for a while and would probably go to Sweet after that to check on him. The on-call doctor met her and smiled, "You know these boys?"

"My cousin is their Commander. I told him I would make sure they are cared for and I wouldn't rest until I knew they were out of the woods."

"I'll watch them while you go to the Chapel," he nodded, aware of the reason she was staying he didn't push her to go home. She went to the Chapel and read Psalms 115-116 and decided to take the bible to Ramey's room. He was still asleep with a vent and machines most people didn't understand, the hum was soothing to her, telling her that he was comfortable. She sat and read quietly and then bowed her head, "Lord, thank you for these three men, thank you for the gift of life and I pray that they heal quickly and have a full recovery. In the bible it says faith as small as a mustard seed can move mountains. I don't want to move mountains God, but I do want to help people be healthy and happy. Please continue to work on these three men and those overseas right now. I pray for Sweet and Ramey, for Kane and Scout. Guide their hearts, their hands, and their steps, help them make it back to us safely and quickly. Thank you for blessing us today and continue to bless these warriors as they mend. In Jesus name—"

"Amen," Doctor Wells leaned in the doorway, "Not every day I hear a prayer warrior for a doctor."

"Being a doctor has shown me that God really is here working because it wasn't my doing to fix Kane and find everything.

You can call it luck, but I call it God every time hands down," she smiled, "How's Sweet and Kane?"

"No progress with Sweet but Kane is sleeping well without support which I agree is a miracle."

"Not every day I hear a big shot doctor agree with me," she smiled and shut the bible, "I better see if Sweet is interested in the next few chapters."

"Why Psalms?" he asked suddenly.

"Because they are uplifting and prayers, I find it calms me down where Judges or Jeremiah gets me fired up," she suppressed a giggle, "Holler if you need me."

"I will, hey just a fair warning, the news heard about the boys being here. Be careful if you decide to go to the hotel tomorrow."

"I may look harmless, but I got steel in my backbone so I'm pretty sure they don't want to mess with me, my patients or their families," she smiled innocently, and he chuckled, "Good to know. I will keep Ramey company for a bit if you don't mind."

"No problem," she moved and went to Sweet's room, she read the next few chapters and heard a slight uptick in his heartbeat. She touched his hand, "Sweet if you can hear me squeeze my hand. Don't panic with the junk all over you I have to make sure you are alright before it can move alright?"

The fingers twitched, and his eyes opened but he didn't react as bad as Kane, he met Skye's eyes and around at all the wires all over him. She raised a finger and called the nurse in, "Sweet has finally decided to grace us with his presence, his vitals show normal, correct?"

"Yes, ma'am," the nurse nodded and smiled to Sweet, "You decided to take a pretty long nap, I have some questions for you."

Skye got a majority of his wires and machines off for a moment and sat watching him. He looked at his arm in a cast and up at the nurse, "Where am I?"

"You are in Nashville at the VA hospital. Can you tell me your name?"

"Charles Sweet, everyone calls me Sweet," he murmured, "Where is Kane and Ramey?"

"Charlie they are in the rooms across from yours, Kane has already been awake, but Gordon likes his sleep," Skye murmured, "Do you remember fifth grade?"

"You were taller than me, I avoid remembering fifth grade just for that reason Skye," his lips twitched, "Where's mom and dad?"

"They are at the hotel because of the visitor hours. I will text them once I know you are alright," she murmured.

"I heard you reading," he relaxed, "Scout said you were going to be here when I woke up."

"You know I wouldn't be anywhere else, I'm going to harass you back to health, so you better make it snappy fast huh?"

"Yes, ma'am," he winced, "Don't make me laugh it hurts pretty bad."

"On a scale of one to ten how bad is your pain, ten being the highest and one being the lowest," the nurse asked ready to assist.

"Depends on if I move or not, or laugh at Skye," he mumbled, "When I move it's about an eight, if I'm sitting still and just breath and relax it is about a four."

"I'll give you some more pain meds and see how it is in a moment," she gave him some more morphine and Skye sat watching him.

"Does it hurt to breath?" she asked watching him.

"Not really, how bad is it, Skye?"

"Not as bad as it could have been," she sighed, "I think you need to sleep with the cannulas on just in case you need it. Your oxygen levels are mediocre at best, okay?"

"You're the boss," he mumbled, "I think I'm going to close my eyes, don't let me sleep all tomorrow I want to see mom and dad, okay?"

"Yes, sir," she saluted as the other doctor came in and glanced at the monitors and nodded to himself.

"You think he's alright?" the nurse asked Dr. Wells.

"I agree with Skye about the oxygen and monitor him closely since he woke up and if he keeps food down tomorrow, I think it's progress. Infection is a key factor now."

Skye agreed and stood with a stretch, "I think I'm headed to Kane and then back to Ramey to finish the night off."

"Alright," Wells agreed and watched her leave the room.

"She's good," the nurse murmured, "Especially as young as she is too."

"I agree," he nodded, "I'm glad she is helping tonight, I needed reminded that miracles can happen."

Kane was up by three and glanced around but seeing Skye with the bible reading silently he cleared his throat and she jumped up and offered him a drink of water and sat back down, "Could you read to me, Skye?"

"What do you want to read?" she asked smiling, "You have 66 different books to choose from you know."

"Funny," his lips twitched remembering not to smile because it hurt, "Whatever you are reading is fine."

Skye read, and the nurse popped her head in and murmured, "Ramey woke up and is starting to panic, Wells said to come help calm him down."

"Sure," Skye smiled to Kane, "Sweet woke earlier."

"Good," he was fighting sleep as it was, and Skye went to Ramey's room and crossed her arms and met his gaze.

"What is your name, Marine," she demanded frowning at him aware they were still trying to take the wires and move them around. Ramey was demanding to see Scout.

"Skye?" he frowned, "Where am I?"

"Nashville now tell me your name," she met his gaze.

"Gordon Ramey," he glanced at the nurse and doctor, "Where is Kane and Sweet? Where is Toby?"

"Kane and Sweet came with you here, as far as Toby I don't know because he's not here. I can call and find out, give me a second," Skye called Scout and put it on speaker, "Hey Skye have they woke up yet?"

"Yes, you are on speaker," she murmured, "Gordon wants to know how Toby is and I couldn't answer him because he's not in my care."

Letters from Home 195

"Toby was hit hard but just had a concussion and broken fingers. Everyone else is alright just fingers broken or bruises, nothing like you and the other two. Get better, Ramey."

"Yes, sir," he sighed, "Can I get some pain relievers my head is killing me."

"Sure," the nurse asked about the scale and he said his head felt like a ten and the nurse moved around. The staff monitored everyone and when the hours came for visitors Skye had already text them all to let them know that everyone had woke and were sleeping again but they didn't have any memory loss. She had them eating hospital food for breakfast and Kane made a face, "I think this is worse than MRE's, Skye."

"Sorry," she shrugged watching the nurse feed him, "If you keep that yummy food down, we can talk about other foods, but you can't get up so remember sometimes you will get sick with the medicine or the nausea."

"Alright," he accepted another bite from the nurse and asked when Martha and the boys were allowed back in and she smiled.

"When you finish breakfast."

"I want to see them," he grumbled eating another bite, "I feel bad when I fell asleep on them."

"Your body dictates when to sleep and when to wake up. Don't worry about it, it's natural, so how is your pain level?"

"Five," he winced, "I catch myself wanting to move and hurting myself."

"Take it a day at a time, Kane," she patted his hand.

"Skye," Nadira had permission to come in and check on them and found a nurse feeding Kane Jell-O.

"Here take over here, make sure he eats all of it and doesn't harass the nurse while I check on Sweet and Ramey before the family are allowed back here," Skye murmured aware it was easier to check them before everyone was crammed in the rooms. She smiled as Sweet accepted a breakfast smoothie from a young nurse on shift. Sweet was always a charmer no matter what he looked like. She stepped out to find Martha and the other families waiting to see them. She glanced at the windows next to the waiting room, "What the heck is that?"

"They heard about the boys being here and the pen pal project in town. They swarmed town too, Zaidee said she's stayed in the back and trying disguises to keep from getting the attention."

"Great," Skye sighed, "Alright guys you have visiting hours, Martha I know it's rough but two people at a time and if he falls asleep let him sleep. They are exhausted and trying to heal which takes a lot out of them. I'm going to lay down for a while and get some sleep here in the doctor's room and be around later to check on them. If you need me find me there."

"Alright," Martha nodded and went in with Ezekiel who wouldn't quit arguing to see Kane first. Nadira came out to find Skye on the phone with Scout and his boss.

"It's come to our attention that the boys drew some attention over there. Avoid any details about the patients but as far as the pen pal thing we are alright with you telling them about the videos and letters and care packages."

"I'm avoiding them at all cost at this point," she sighed, "Scout who was the girl in your class that went to work at Nashville?"

"Journalist? Uh, Lettie Joseph, why?"

"If we are going to answer questions I'm doing it with one person not a whole crowd," she grumbled, "Lack of sleep, I'll let Nadira handle it."

"Fun," Nadira sighed.

"Have fun and get some sleep, Skye," Scout sounded amused.

Skye went to lie down and slept until Nadira touched her arm, "Skye?"

"Hm," she rubbed the grit from her eyes and noticed they were swollen from lack of sleep, "Time is it?"

"Almost four pm," Nadira murmured.

"Oh," she stretched and stood up with a groan as her body aches made themselves known.

"Lettie said it would be awesome to get the scoop, but she'd be murdered before making it to the door. She put together a press release for six pm at the hotel. She said she would help you field the questions and lay down the rules to keep from them railroading you."

"I need to call the Marine headquarters and speak to someone as well."

"I already did," Nadira had done some research online while Skye slept to anticipate her moves and what needed done as well as talked to Martha and the other family members about how this usually worked. Martha had known a few women that had dealt with it and found an old acquaintance to help Skye, "I have someone going to meet you and escort you to the hotel, so you can get a shower and get ready."

"Someone?" she frowned, "Who?"

"Major Thompson," Nadira waited for the name to sink in but Skye's mind was sluggish and all she wanted was more sleep as she yawned hugely behind her hand.

"I don't know him," Skye shrugged, "How's our patients?"

"Sleeping a lot but everything looks good, Kane's oxygen has went down a bit, but Charlie's oxygen has improved," Nadira studied her, "Take a round to see for yourself and then you are going to the hotel."

"Bossy, bossy," Skye gave a sleepy smile and went to see Sweet, he was sleeping, and his mom was holding his hand. Skye checked his charts and looked at Lori, his mom, "Has he been up often enough?"

"He's been awake off and on, a few minutes here and there, they just gave him meds again."

"Alright, I'm going to the hotel for a shower and I'll be back tonight," she knew they were worried, but she couldn't do more for him. She looked to Lori, "Do you want me to pray with you guys?"

"I think we should all pray," Kane's voice sounded from across the hall, he sounded stronger which was a blessing to her ears, "Together."

"I think that's an order," Skye glanced at the nurses at their station monitoring and watching as everyone went to Kane's room, Ramey and Sweet were still sleeping peacefully, "You ladies can join if you want."

"Thanks," one smiled as the other shook her head and said, "I'll watch the other two rooms while you pray. Thank you."

Skye went to the room and looked at Kane, "You want to pray?"

"I can start you can finish," he murmured waiting for her to nod, she smiled waiting for him to begin, "Dear lord, thank you for giving us another day to see our family and friends. Thank you for the doctors and nurses who kept us alive to do so, continue to bless their hands and guide them. I'm not great with words but you know my heart. I pray for the men still over there, you know the situation they are in, let their aim be true, give them a sound mind, guard their hearts, and give them dreams of home. I pray you surround them in reassurance that you have them and that you are with them."

His hand squeezed Skye's hand and she smiled, "God, you have told us we are fearfully and wonderfully made, continue to guide our steps, guard our hearts, our thoughts, our minds, guide us in everything. Give these families rest, give these three men swift healing, and I pray for the other families of the Marines and soldiers overseas, you know every name, you know every heart, if they don't know you touch them, if they know you give them peace of mind, and God wrap your arms around them, let them feel the love and comfort you have to offer. Give the men and women fighting peace of mind and their leaders' guidance and discernment in every decision. I pray for our president, I pray for the world, God we all need you, I pray you provide exactly what we need when we need it. I pray you show us a little more of you every day and I pray that we continue to get a closer relationship with you. Thank you for the amazing people in this hospital and everyone here for continuing to show me miracles can happen. Continue to work through all of us in Jesus name, amen."

Kane met her gaze, "You inspire me, Skye."

"You are full of surprises yourself there, dad," she grinned as he groaned, "I'm not that old!"

"I have a press release to get to," Skye tussled Lane's hair, "Watch him for me alright?"

"Okay," Lane's back straightened with purpose and his young face set in determined lines.

"Nothing but hospital food," she told Kane who sighed.

"Now you're just being mean," he shook his head.

"No, I'm keeping you from regretting it later," she turned serious.

She checked on Ramey and Sweet one more time before leaving and finding Thompson standing in the waiting room, she froze surprised and was reminded of the late night with the Miles family. He stood still, looking down at his phone, not noticing her freeze at the sight of him. She collected herself and stepped forward to greet him. "Major."

"Ma'am," he smiled, "You ready to go?"

"As ready as I can be," she sighed, "I have no idea where I'm going though so I hope Nadira covered everything."

"Yes, ma'am, I have the address and your car keys. The reporters are still outside so we are going out the side and around," he motioned, and she followed at his side pressure in her chest, like a weight with the stress, hitting her hard. Her hands shook, and she took a steading breath as they came to the door.

The hotel was an expensive one by looks alone with large pillars in the front. They pulled around back and into the elevator, Thompson had the room key for Skye. He carried her bag and led her to the room. "You have an hour to get ready and then I will be briefing you."

"Okay," she nodded, "I'll be about twenty minutes."

He was surprised she told him to sit and relax while she went to the restroom to take a shower. She French braided her hair and came out in dress shirt and slacks. She had flats on and although it was a little wrinkled, she didn't care. She sat and opened a mirror as she did her makeup because she wasn't about to look that bad on any TV. She saw him studying her, "Do I look half human now?"

"I thought you looked fine before," he smiled, "You've had a rough few days from the sounds of it."

"So, what can I say and what should I not say?"

"As far as what they are doing you can't say anything, not that Scout has told you anything. I contacted him and his boss to confirm what he has told you," he leaned forward. He could see the tired rings under her eyes that he hadn't seen before. She inspired him with her dedication to her family and friends.

"As far as the letters and videos tell them everything you want to tell. All the girls have been in touch with Nadira and they all said to deal with it, but they weren't about to come out of hiding. Adelina said if you need anything she's coming to visit tomorrow."

"Well let's go down and get this ball rolling," she sighed, "Lettie here yet?"

"She is," Major Thompson agreed, "She's surprised you had Nadira contact her."

"She went to school with Scout, I wanted someone that knew our town to understand we didn't want bombarded with questions," Skye set her makeup down on the table and stood with another stretch feeling a little better but really wanting to sleep. She stifled another yawn and the Major chuckled.

"Alright, let's see if we can keep these reporters from asking too many questions," he walked next to her and led her to the banquet area the hotel had set up for the press conference. Lettie looked shocked to see Skye there early.

"Hey!" her hug was tight, unlike most big city people who gave empty hugs.

"Hey," Skye smiled, "Nadira said you both set this up and you were going to help me keep from getting tongue-tied?"

"You will do fine, I laid down the law and will be right here for you, I have a few questions as well so go have a seat, Rick there will get you set up with the microphone, so we can all hear you and save your voice okay."

"Major Thompson as well," Skye added, and Rick agreed motioning them to the seats on stage. There were three and Lettie sat to the far side. Once the microphones were in place Lettie asked for a microphone check on them both.

"This isn't awkward at all," Thompson smiled to Skye trying to ease the tension he noticed around her eyes. Skye hated to be the center of the attention so doing this stressed her more than surgeries did.

"I'd rather do a million surgeries than do this, less intimidating," she admitted hearing the boom of her voice over the system.

"Everyone come in and settle in, cameramen at the back," Lettie instructed, "I'm Lettie, I will be facilitating the press release. It looks different than any other press release because our friends have been on their feet for a few days and need some rest. You all have been told the rules so once you've settled, we will start."

The murmuring fell silent as everyone sat with recorders and notepads out. Skye was amazed such a huge room could look so tiny with so many people. The hardwood floor and paneling shone with care knowing this was huge publicity for their hotel as well. The ball room quieted to the point you could hear the quiet hiss of the air conditioning.

"I'm sitting with Doctor Skyelar Hamilton and Major Jared Thompson. My name is Lettie Joseph your host tonight. So Skye, I've known you for years, but our friends tell me you met Major Thompson recently and trusted him. Tell me how you know him."

"As some of you are aware Elizabethtown Tennessee has had tragedy hit already this year. Major Thompson was the serviceman who delivered the notification with Chaplain Landon King to my house."

"One of the hardest days I've had this year," Thompson agreed, "Skye was next of kin for one of our Marines. She was aware of what it meant that we were there, and I panicked when she asked which Marine I was there to deliver the notification. Most families have one Marine they worry about but here was a young lady standing there holding it together for two."

"Preparing for the news, Johnny Miles had passed, and I was named secondary next of kin because I was as close as siblings to him. He told me that he didn't want his parents to see an unfamiliar face pulling up in the official car. Major Thompson and I helped the family that week and have stayed in touch ever since."

"So now months later, the same platoon has three injured and sent state-side for surgeries and what?" Lettie asked.

"The platoon has had two others before this sent home with injuries. I believe it was a few weeks ago?" she looked to Thompson for verification which he shook his head and raised three fingers.

"Three weeks ago, my days have blurred together sorry, I received a call from my family member telling me that one of the men demanded me as his doctor and to get to Nashville."

Letters from Home

"What you need to understand is that although she is a family member to a Marine, her Marine is a Platoon Commander and because he's not married, Skye is the point of contact for the families here in the states," Thompson murmured to Lettie realizing everyone heard as Skye smiled at his flushing face. He hated that Skye was being bombarded with news crews because it was Nashville and not Elizabethtown but he also wanted them to know what an amazing young lady she was too.

"So, when your cousin called what did you do?" Lettie asked. Skye explained, and Lettie raised a hand, "Time out, who is Nadira and why did you call her?"

"Nadira is one of the pen pals, one that wrote to one of the wounded here in the hospital," she nodded, "I called her to tell her that I wasn't going to be at work and she said she'd be on my porch in a minute. She contacted the families to make sure they had rides before we left town and we arrived at the hospital before the men."

"Tell us about these letters, what started it?"

"That's a long story," Skye smiled and fought tears suddenly, "And an emotional one."

"Take your time," Lettie reached over and took her hand.

"Johnny grew up with my cousin and I, my grandpa was explaining a box of letters the boys found in the attic and how my grandma wrote to him when he was in the Marines. I…I was made to swear to write to them when they went into the Marines. They knew from an early age that's what they wanted to do. When Johnny passed the platoon showed homesickness and were depressed. Most the boys from town are in the same platoon and deployed together which is rare but makes them a tighter knit group. When that happened, it was suggested to start pen pals, my cousin contacted me and

Letters from Home

said his team leads suggested pen pals and that I always wrote him, and it started with my friends."

"Now it's expanded, correct? Into a video edition?" Lettie smiled.

"It's one thing to send pictures and letters, we decided to send a video of home to the boys of our hometown. We told them it might not be their home, but it was America and that counted. We continued letters, some of them were our daily routines and asking what they wanted from the pen pal project. Alara wrote her pen pal about a failed DIY project and asked for hobbies. Unbeknownst to any of us that her pen pal is an adrenaline junkie who loves heights and she talked us into sky diving and rock climbing."

"You are afraid of heights, right?" Lettie grinned, "I bet that was interesting."

"I heard this story, your first parachute stalled right?" Thompson asked.

"Yeah, needless to say I've avoided the sky at all cost, I don't even look up when I walk outside," she chuckled, "The videos were a hit, we went across the US to help family members who didn't know how to run the technology to make a video. We sent individual DVDs to the whole platoon."

"Who did all the recording?" Lettie asked.

"Adelina," Skye smiled, "She's planning to go to college next year for a degree in the field. She was a Godsend, she continues to surprise us, and she asked…more like begged for the guys to send a video back. It was hard for most the girls to write because we didn't have a face to go with a name and only so much came in a letter."

"We have a question from the audience, well quite a few but one at a time," Lettie motioned to the front row.

Letters from Home

"Can you tell us about your pen pals?"

"Not really, only that one misses the mountains around his home and another misses a cute basset hound," she smiled, "Our men are fighting a war and their families want to stay out of the newspapers and news. The guys are serving their country and it's another deployment for most of them. They love their country and miss their family."

"Major Thompson I have a question for you," the man stood in a suit, "Having met Ms. Hamilton and the community what can you tell us about how they are similar or different than other notifications you've given."

"The community and Skye are totally different from most my notifications. It might be because it's a small community but as soon as the community heard the press release the entire community was at the Miles house for support whether that was a hug or just a silent vigil. They stand together, they mourn together, it's a quiet community that likes the peace of a small town. Most are veterans that served and now their children are serving in a branch of the military. It's just another generation doing what they feel is right, to fight injustice and serve however the government decides. I've never met someone who could tell me where everyone in town was at any one time except for Skye. She's an emergency doctor there, she recently became VA certified and when a family goes camping, she can pinpoint where exactly they are camping and take you right to them," he flashed an amused smile to Skye who smiled back. "Ms. Hamilton is an inspiration. She goes above and beyond her responsibility and loves the people she helps. She is that person you call when you need help and you know she will be there for you day or night. She's an amazing young lady and I'm blessed to have met her."

Letters from Home

Lettie smiled seeing Skye flush at such praise, she motioned to another hand up.

"What made you become a VA doctor?" the lady asked, Skye realized they'd be there a bit.

"Sorry do we have any water?" she asked Lettie who held up a bottle of Ice Mountain and she took a quick drink and cleared her throat, "Our community is small but with so many veterans in the community they had to travel almost three hours to a VA hospital, this one is closest to our town. Our hospital is working toward becoming more oriented to the veterans as well. I like dealing with children and shots and emergencies but if a vet has an emergency three hours isn't fast enough to get to the hospital. I wanted to give them something closer. It's my way of serving my country by serving its military. All our doctors agree."

Hours later, millions of questions they were wrapping up and Skye touched Lettie's hand, "Please remember that our community sees this as another day in the normal routine. It may be news to you but to us it's our way of encouraging and helping our boys. Please remember to be courteous and stop at the stop signs, the pen pals want to stay anonymous and we should respect that."

Her phone rang, and she pulled the microphone off and answered, "Hello?"

"Skye the boys refuse to leave until you get here," Martha murmured worried seeing the nurses watching them.

"We are coming now," she looked to Thompson, "We need to head back."

"Let's go," he nodded pulling his microphone off and following her to the door. Skye sighed as she sat in the passenger seat. Thompson called his boss, "I think it went well sir…yes, sir…I will."

Skye called Scout and closed her eyes, "Press release looked like fun, cousin."

"You already saw it?" she frowned confused.

"Yes," he nodded having sat with his boss and colleagues, "You kept it aimed at town and you and that's all good."

"Any word on when you are getting to come home?"

"No," he sighed.

Skye fought tears and thickly stated, "I miss your face, Scout."

Chapter 10
Adelina's surprise

The week went by without incident for Skyelar, Adelina's aunt took her to them, to stay with them to help watch the boys since Nadira went back to work. At the end of the week Skyelar met the boys' eyes, "Your dad is healing nicely, and I have to go save some other people's lives. Call me if he changes but he's on the road to recovery and he's out of the woods. Sweet and Ramey as well."

"Thank you, Skyelar," Martha murmured, "We will need to figure out where to stay from here right?"

"Actually," Adelina smiled, "I might have called around and gotten another week free. It is totally a God thing when I explained who I was they were like as long as you do a piece on our hotel and publicize it while you are here, we agree to give rooms to the families for free."

"What kind of piece are you talking about?" Skye frowned. Adelina could see the tired lines and how worn down she was, she lost more weight which made Adelina worry too. She knew Skye was so invested in the boys that she'd starve to death before realizing she was hungry. Adelina didn't have that issue she could eat all the time and still be hungry. She flashed a smile, if she could take something off Skye's plate maybe it would help Skye relax a bit.

"I have to do a video for them, same hotel, same rooms," Adelina stood and stepped to her, "Don't worry, Skye, I'll take care of them and when they are ready to come home, we will be there for your inspection."

"Alright," she nodded, "Kane keep them out of trouble."

"I thought I would be relieved of duty when I got state-side," he sighed mournfully. His bruising was lighter and the

Letters from Home 210

swelling on his face was down, he looked good considering five days ago he was knocking on death's door.

"Do you need a ride, Skye?" Adelina asked.

"Nadira is coming to get me since she has my car. She is driving me home," she yawned, "My bag is packed so I've just got to tell Sweet and Ramey."

"Thanks Skye," Ezekiel met her eyes with his big blue ones. He was the reason Skye stayed so long, to make him feel better but nothing happened and so it was time to go home. She told the doctors goodbye and the nurses she came to know well. They all smiled and promised to look after her children for her. She laughed as she went to Sweet's room, "I have to go back to my normal job, you are in good hands and I will see you in a couple weeks. Do what they tell you or I get a phone call and I will be back up here making your head ache."

"Yes, ma'am," he was serious not taking the joke. She went to Ramey and told him that she'd see him soon. He agreed, and she went to the door to find Nadira there putting her bag in the car. Adelina watched it all from the hall. She had her work cut out for her, Scout had called her and told her that the girls needed to plan a small party. With Skye home it would be harder, but Adelina had most of it planned.

Adelina had called Marjorie about rooms and Zaidee said she'd call a friend to grill out. She called Serabeth about alcohol, "I'm not old enough remember."

Serabeth laughed and said, "If they want alcohol, they can buy it themselves or Rashel will."

Adelina had four weeks to make everything perfect, the whole town knew not to tell Skye on pain of death. Kane and the boys should be healed up by then and everyone had time to get home see everyone and then arrive in Elizabethtown.

The boys were excited to be actors for her video and she recorded them walking to the room, going in and relaxing, swimming in the pool. It kept them busy as Martha dealt with other things. Adelina had sent quite a few videos to the boys since Skye was busy, she was surprised that Skye wrote every day to M&M and sent it with the hospital's mail. Adelina sat at the laptop and played the video.

Zooming in on the large hotel with a car pulling into the valet it read, **In the big city you can make it big in the music city of America, but can you get this kind of service at any hotel?**

The hardwood floor in the hallways following the boys as they went to the hotel. Adelina's voice rose quietly, "Stay where the big stars stay when they come to town. Dolly, Led Zeppelin, you name it they've been here walking these very halls. The hotel is close to downtown, so you can walk to the main attractions. They offer anything and everything you can imagine. Don't believe me, meet the staff, call them and they will confirm my story."

The staff members stood at attention behind the desk smiling and one answered the phone with a wink at the camera. When she backed up and showed the ballroom and swimming pool. She showed all the highlights around the area and faded out on the beginning picture of the outside of the hotel again.

Adelina sent it to the manager with a letter asking what he thought. If he wanted something different, she would do it. She went to the hospital and recorded Kane and the guys going through therapy together. When it was over Kane met her gaze, "You are recording us?"

"Yes, sir," she smiled.

"I want to tell them something," he straightened and looked at Martha, "Give me a moment babe."

"Sure sweetie, you want a drink or food?"

"Skye said no real food," he rolled his eyes, "I'd do anything for a steak and mashed potatoes."

"Skye is your doctor and until you can walk without help to get to the restroom, I would say you aren't going anywhere to get your own," she smiled.

He sighed and looked at the camera, "Hey guys, as you can tell we are doing better every day. Skye comes on her days off to check on us. I know I'm missed because I can just hear the pranks from here so be good and listen to your team leads or I'm going to have to make the staff send me back to yell at you."

He scratched his chin, "Rumor has it that you are coming home as soon as the next group is settled. Skye and everyone here is praying it's soon, the other family members from Elizabethtown have come to visit us a few times here, asking how their boys are and making sure we are taken care of which is awesome."

"Are you going to tell them the news?" Adelina asked smiling.

"Martha has informed me that we are selling the house. She had three offers the first day on market and we are moving to Elizabethtown. The boys aren't extremely excited since they want to play hockey, but a rink is about thirty minutes away, so we can make it work. Movers are delivering our stuff to a storage unit to be shipped down here in the next few days. Since it will be a while before my leg heals and it's good enough to walk, she said now is as good a time as any to move because I can't argue. I love you brothers and I can't wait to hear the news you are finally home too. I wish I wasn't this bad and could still be there to watch your back, but someone had to make sure Sweet and Ramey did what they were told and eat the hospital food.... word to the wise—stay safe because hospital food is worse than MRE's."

"I'm going to go find Sweet and Ramey and see if they want to record," she smiled seeing he was worn out. He nodded and noticed Martha at the door waiting for him to finish.

"Where are the boys?" he asked fighting to keep his eyes open.

"Nadira is off today and she took them to a local ice-skating rink to skate for a while. She said they were making her tired as much energy as they had," Martha grinned.

Adelina hurried through recording the other two and jumped in the car, calling Nadira about the rink, she explained where they were, and Adelina walked in to find a group of boys with them playing hockey. Lane, Case, and Ezekiel were part of one team and they were kicking butt. She recorded them for a while and then went back to the hospital.

In the waiting room there was a desk that Adelina used to edit her videos, she had an audience when the boys came back. They watched her work in silence, she straightened and recorded on her laptop camera, "Hey guys! So, I think this is Episode....142, don't quote me on it, Letters from Home Edition. I've been staying in Nashville to help Martha and the families and working with the local hotel on advertising. I also promised Skye I'd make sure Kane ate his steamed broccoli which is definitely a fight with the big guy," she rubbed her eyes, "I've also been planning some awesomeness for Skye's surprise. I have the nurses and doctors in on it here as well as the post office in town because she doesn't know you are heading to debriefing next week. We are trying hard to keep your mail straight to get to where you are going. A few families that don't live near your homes are planning to travel on vacation to see you in Elizabethtown. It's going to be an epic party and we aren't publicizing any of it so hopefully by then the news teams will stop following Skye around and quit being peaking toms."

The camera showed the camera crew outside the window chilling out, "We've learned that the emergency bay is the best exit strategy so if you decide to visit these boys remember that because some Marines and military men get bombarded with questions about if they know these guys or where they fought. It's devastating to watch the guys go through it. You can see them struggle to hold in the sudden feeling of threat and keep from tensing up. When we see a car pull up one of Kane's boys will run around the back and get their attention because the news isn't allowed around the side of the building which helps."

She glanced at the boys, "Anything to add boys?"

"We've all been praying for you and when Skye isn't here, we've been praying for her. She's stretched thin and with news crews following her around she's stressed. She's exhausted and she looks like the wind could blow her over," Case murmured.

"Skye will be fine once she knows the guys are home safe, she's just got a hard job that keeps her awake, boys. I told you not to worry. Now I think Nadira has a project for you so shoo."

She watched them walk away and looked at the camera. To be honest she was stretched thin and they hit the nail on the head that she's stressed with the news following her around. The local police have been stopping them from going to her house or the hospital and keep them back. Summertime meant she got a lot more emergency calls, so Skye didn't get much sleep. Not that Adelina would tell them and make them worry. Alara and Nadira take care of Skye and make sure she's taking care of herself. "Alara and Nadira said just to get your butts home soon so she has one less thing on her plate. The pen pals have the news crews taken care of by calling the police to keep the news from coming and interrupting their peaceful town. The police like the camera time so all is well except Jonah—the Deputy said he was kind of upset he hadn't had to use his taser on anyone."

Adelina sent the video to the correct address of the base where they were going to be debriefed. She found Skye pulling in and looked confused as another person got out of the passenger seat. She watched them come through the back and around to the waiting room. "Adelina," Skye found her on her laptop.

"Hey Skye, who is with you?" Adelina glanced at the boys who were hidden on the other side of the waiting room talking and coloring. Skye wouldn't notice what they were doing.

"I'm Lance Eldridge," he held up his hand, "I'm a professor at Chattanooga University. Everyone in the industry has heard of the young lady who sends videos to the Marine Platoon. I came to offer you a place with us."

"Oh!" Adelina stood aware she stood in some ratty t-shirt and sweatpants, "Sorry I wasn't expecting to meet anyone today."

"No worries," he grinned, "Can we talk?"

"Sure," she nodded.

"Could you show me some of your portfolio? I checked with the university and they said you haven't applied."

"I was planning to take a year off," Adelina admitted, "I was planning to work over that year and make money to save for college."

"Instead, you've been making videos for our guys overseas," he nodded seeing her face flush.

She opened the first video she found and smiled as the basset hound echoed over the laptop speakers. She loved that video, "This is of one of the pen pals' family and their dog. He had written that although while he was home, he was constantly yelling for Dude to shut up he missed the dog desperately. Skye and I took a road trip and went across the country to get videos for the families."

"She said you have done at least a hundred that she was aware of in less than four months?" he was impressed with her.

"The videos we sent at the start were just of us and then family members were sending us videos of their families, those that couldn't make one we went around to video and that was well over sixty in less than a month. They were short videos of anywhere from 5 to 10 minutes. I think I'm on 142, I just finished and sent it. Most the time it's news of family or updates on their buddies here. They had four new guys and so I sent a welcome video and got in touch with their families to send to them as well. I get videos from families consistently of updates and send them."

"That's awesome!" he shook his head, "And your software is good. I wanted to see if you were interested in starting in August. It may be a breeze for you since you are comfortable making videos and know most of the software."

"I would love that but unfortunately I can't afford college right now," she met his gaze, "In a year I hope to be a little better off financially."

"Would it help that Chattanooga University has a few scholarships and grants for you?"

"How is that possible when I haven't applied?"

Letters from Home 217

"Let's just say some colleges and universities will fund you just to have bragging rights to get you, I don't think you know how popular you really are," he smiled, "Your great-aunt is raising you as a single parent, that means you can get federal grants and scholarships, I'm assuming your school didn't explain much on this?"

"Not really, small towns where not a lot of people go to college," she shrugged, "I told them I was taking a year off and wasn't in half the meetings so maybe I missed something."

"Well, I'm here to help you out. I took the liberty of working with your aunt yesterday to fill out the information. This is what you received from FAFSA; the university is willing to cover the rest of the expenses. I'm working on a video pen pal project at the school as well. The Platoon Commander and his boss have agreed that it was a perfect way to remind them what they are fighting for and gave them a piece of home. We want to expand what you've done here, Adelina."

She looked up at Skye who smiled, "You said college was what you wanted Adelina, and this sounds awesome. Your aunt has had four other colleges reach out to her, but this is the best offer so far."

"It means my college is paid for completely until I graduate, and I don't pay anything back?" she looked to Eldridge surprised.

"Yes," he nodded, "Your aunt even applied to the college for you. The only thing is that you will have to pay for books and software, you already have a video camera so until junior year you won't need anything else."

"Okay," Adelina looked at Skye, "Chattanooga was on my list, I loved the campus, and everyone was so nice."

Skye saw her wheels turning, she smiled, "You still need to have a graduation party, you were too busy going to your friends' graduation parties you didn't have one. Most the time people give money then and you will have time to get the money."

"Then yes," Adelina smiled excited, "When can I get classes scheduled?"

"Now, I came out here to make sure I helped you get ready and everything was in order. If you play your cards right, you can graduate early since you have a huge portfolio. I want you to continue to make videos while you wait for August to come around. I don't need Marines angry with me for stealing their video master."

Adelina giggled, "I will, I promise."

"Good," he sat and gave her a letter with her email and password. She read the welcome letter and glanced up to see Skye had went back to check on the guys. Adelina set up her schedule surprised that most of her English classes transferred to Chattanooga and her gen eds were easy classes. When she finished, she looked to Eldridge aware he taught one of her classes, "So you came all the way here to find me?"

"We are excited to have you, Adelina," he smiled.

"I have to record this," she reached up and grabbed her recorder and turned it to Eldridge, "Tell the platoon what just happened, Mr. Eldridge."

"Adelina has been sought by Chattanooga University to join our ranks and classes for a film degree. She has agreed to join us in August and I will be one of her teachers in the fall."

"How did you find me?" she asked curiously.

"Well, I sought out your guardian who helped me answer some questions about you. I had heard about your video master from many people and it's all over the news that a high school graduate was sending videos to a Marine Platoon. A bunch of colleges have been clamoring to get in touch with her. When I asked where Adelina was her great-aunt said she was making sure the injured Marines were eating veggies like the doctor ordered. Doctor Hamilton was headed this way and I hitched a ride with her."

"Well thank you for finding me, I look forward to August!"

She stopped and put it on the computer to work on, she recorded herself on her laptop with him watching what she did, "Hey boys! I have some crazy news! God works in mysterious ways for sure! I just saw Skye walk in with someone and I thought who in the world until Skye found me in the waiting room with the boys. Professor Lance Eldridge will answer the questions from here!"

It cut to him answering and she came back on, "With the education I hope doors open for me to continue to video and help people. I can't wait for you all to get this! I got to look at books and start getting ahead of classes. Don't think this stops the videos I just want to make sure I don't fall behind! Until next time, Letters from Home Edition 143…I think."

She winked and burnt the disc to send quickly. She found the boys still coloring and warned them, "Don't let Skye see that, Lane."

"I won't," he flashed a smile as he helped Ezekiel make an e in Welcome. Case was reading a book to make origami style decorations it seemed because he kept referencing the book as he used scissors to cut the paper. Adelina bounced excitedly, and Eldridge chuckled, "I look forward to this semester with you, Adelina."

"I do too!" she smiled, "Thank you for looking me up."

"I want to talk to the news and let them know we will be having our own celebrity this year. When Skye's ready I will be done," he stood and walked out the front door and smiled with a wave.

Adelina watched him smile and wave and start talking. She turned on the TV to see what he said as she looked up books. He explained the plan for the film department and asked who better to help them succeed than to recruit the first young lady that started it.

Chapter 11
Home

Skye had been going back and forth between hospitals for three weeks checking on the guys and keeping up with work. Talking to M&M and Scout both often and relaxing knowing it calmed down a bit for a moment. She had helped Martha find a rental as she bought property just outside of town to build on. Martha checked with the Tennessee standards for becoming a realtor and took the correct steps. She would have to travel but it was worth it. Kane and the others came home soon after that. The pen pals helped them move into the rental and Adelina recorded and helped as well. Skye got a call about an emergency and went to the hospital with Alara who got the same call. Kane promised Nadira would keep him in line as they moved. He was still sore, and he was still favoring his one leg that had fractured.

Late that night Skye went to the house and made a pot of tea. A tap hit the door two hours later when she was about to go to bed. She opened the door to find two Marines with their bags at their feet. She froze seeing Scout, "You didn't tell me you were coming home!"

She swiped her tears away and gave him a bear hug, "Miss me, Skyelar?"

"Yeah," she stepped back to study him, seeing a new scar on his cheek and cocked her head, "You forget to duck again?"

"Something like that," he froze as she touched the thin line and then her attention landed on the man beside him.

"I recognize you from the video we got," she frowned, "What's your name?"

"Derek Mercer," he watched her.

"You called him M&M," Scout told her.

"About time I get a name," she chuckled and gave him a hug, "Are you hungry, when did you get over here?"

"We landed a week ago but were released to go home yesterday. I hope you don't mind Derek staying with us, his sister and her boys are headed this way to meet him," Scout murmured.

"Of course not," she shook her head, "I can cook, or we can get something if you are hungry."

She looked them over and noticed Derek had a few scars as well, she looked to Scout and hugged him again, "I can't believe you're finally home."

She swiped her eyes and gave a happy laugh at seeing his beat-up old truck, he was safe at last.

"We aren't hungry, just tired," he murmured studying her tired eyes, "When's the last time you slept anyway, Skye? You look tired."

"I had a late shift; I have to be up in a few hours. Let's get you both settled, we have time to talk tomorrow," she swiped her eyes and said, "Did you drive straight through with the boys too?"

"Most the way through, we stopped late last night and drove the rest, Dylan's car had trouble, so we had to fix it before we could get here." Mercer murmured, naming another Elizabethtown Marine, one that Skye knew since kindergarten.

"Leave it to him," Skye laughed, "Well Derek come on, I'll show you to your room, and you can rest."

She picked up his bag and Scout's bag and went upstairs without seeing their shared look of surprise, those were heavy bags and she didn't hesitate to go into hospitality mode. She set Scout's in his room and told him to wait for a moment she had to change the sheets and went to the room next to his and set Derek's rucksack down and grabbed sheets and made the bed up fast. She turned to find Scout and Derek at the door watching her. She looked at Derek, "Make yourself at home, if you need anything don't be afraid to wake me up or Scout. I will be getting up early, so I will be quiet to keep from waking you up but don't worry if you hear someone moving around, I have weird hours."

"Thanks Skye," Derek nodded.

"You know you changed the sheets because you told me you cleaned and dusted my room last week, don't worry about it, Skye get some sleep," Scout touched her cheek studying her.

"If you need anything yell," she hugged him hard again and studied his face, "This isn't a dream, is it?"

"No," he shook his head, "Come on, Doc, you need sleep."

He walked her to her room and found she hadn't changed a thing for the year he was away, it looked the same as it had when she was little. She had a light blue comforter that matched the walls, she never kept toys in her room and her bookcase was the only thing that changed it was bigger and had thicker books next to her window seat, "Night cousin."

"Night," she smiled, "I love you."

"Love you more," he chuckled and kissed her forehead. He caught sight of a big shoebox next to her bed but didn't reach for it. He went to the door and checked on Derek one more time. "You good, Mercer?"

"Yes, sir," he nodded sitting on the comfortable bed, "Thank you for letting me stay."

"Your parents coming with your sister?" he asked.

Letters from Home   224

"Yes sir," he nodded, "This cut it close considering the party is tomorrow."

"I'm glad everyone was headed this way anyway. Quinn called Kane and Adelina met everyone at the hotel. Marjorie has everyone settled. Let's get some sleep."

"Yes, sir," Derek noticed a small bible under the bedside table and as Scout shut the door, he opened it to find it was an old bible, opening the front cover he saw Skyelar Hamilton's name written roughly as if she just learned to write. A small letter sat there as well, and he opened it.

There is a bible in every bedroom for you if you can't sleep. I know it's a different culture over there and although I never experienced it, I continuously pray for you. Get some sleep, you deserve a rest, crack the window, and listen to the crickets—it helps Scout when he is fresh off the plane. Feel free to make yourself at home, you can always wake me if you need anything and yes, the kitchen is always open.

--Skye

Behind that letter another nearly fell to the floor and Derek frowned.

Hey,

You may not know me, but I've slept in this room for years, growing up with Skye and Scout. As the years passed, I find it harder and harder to sleep. Skye doesn't look at these books only makes sure they are in easy reach for those that need them. If you can't sleep, I understand, you are waiting for another wake-up call to arm yourself and fight. Dread and weariness make it hard to close your eyes because you remember everything like a video on replay, a nightmare you lived through and others didn't, but this book helps. Skye taught me that. So, if you don't know where to start you can

Letters from Home 225

start at my favorite, it makes me relax and calms me down. Psalms 91. We don't always know what God's plans are but if you know your own heart you aren't afraid to face what's next. God bless and Semper Fi.

--Johnny Miles

Derek held his breath forcing the emotions he tried desperately to bury to quit bubbling to the surface. He turned to Psalms 91 and laid back, the lamp gave a soft light to read by as he tried to relax. He didn't remember falling asleep as he read it again.

Skye's phone beeped, and she answered it quickly, "Hello?"

"We had a call from Oakland hospital, an apartment fire multiple injury, all hands onboard for this one," Dr. Walsh sounded tired.

"I'm headed that way."

She stepped into the hall to find Scout standing without a shirt on, "What's going on?"

"Apartment fire, I am called in, Oakland is overloaded and sending patients to other hospitals," she whispered aware their guest was sleeping, "Go back to bed, Scout."

"I'll see you later," he murmured.

"You bet," she hadn't even brushed her hair she tossed it up and slipped her shoes on as she walked out the door. Scout turned to see Derek still in his uniform still.

"Did you fall asleep yet?" he asked yawning.

"For a bit," he nodded, "I'm going back to bed, sir."

"Me too, night, Derek."

They went back to bed and realized Skye only had an hour of sleep. Derek smelled bacon the next morning and followed his

Letters from Home

nose as he went downstairs. Scout came down soon after and froze seeing Serabeth with Evie there. Both guys had pants on, but no shirts and they were surprised she was there, "Skye called me this morning to let me know that I have no babysitter for Evie this morning unless I could talk you two into agreeing. I made a welcome home breakfast!"

"Hey Sera," Scout yawned and stretched, "Hey Evie."

"It's just until noon," Sera promised, "Mom will come pick her up then."

"Sure, you like to fish right, Evie?" Scout smiled.

"Yeah!" Evie giggled.

They ate and went to the pond in silence, Derek caught the first fish and asked Evie if she wanted to kiss it before he let it loose. She crinkled her little nose and shook her head violently, "Ew!"

"It might turn into a prince," Derek held the fish as it wriggled.

"That's frogs!" Evie shook her head again, "Aunt Sera said all the frog prince have been taken so not to kiss them."

"Smart of Aunt Sera," Scout grinned, slowly relaxing, having caught his eyes watching the farm around them like something would explode or happen here. He knew better, hearing a car door he stood and turned finding Zane Wolf with Quinn and realized Zane was Shawn's (another Marine lost to war) daughter's godfather, but Zane had never met her.

"It looks like we have some more friends to help us fish," Derek murmured standing as well and looked at Evie, "You sure you don't want to kiss it?"

"I'm positive," Evie pursed her lips and crinkled her nose again.

Letters from Home

Zane came up and sat next to Derek and glanced down at Evie, "Well who's this fishing girl?"

"I'm Evie," she looked to Scout, "Throw it for me?"

"Sure," Scout tossed her hook out, having to bait it because she refused to touch a worm.

"Genevieve Sabine Miller," Evie looked at Zane, "Aunt Sera says it's a mouthful so Evie."

Zane glanced at Scout to see if this was the right kid, he hadn't meant to meet her without grandma or aunt around. "Evie what's your daddy's name?"

"Shawn Dylan Miller," she looked at Zane, "Aunt Sera says he went to see Jesus."

Zane nodded slowly and looked at Derek, "You catch anything?"

"I caught a fish, but Evie here didn't want to kiss it to see if it turned into a prince," Derek nodded.

"That only happens for frogs," Quinn laughed.

"Like I'd know that, I don't need a prince," Derek scowled, and they all erupted into laughter as Evie squealed and took off running backward pulling the fish on her line out of the water in the process. They all laughed as Scout caught the line and told her to come back. She turned and raced back looking at the fish.

"Wow it's huge!" she looked up at Scout.

"We need a picture of that, but you need to touch it since it's your first one, it brings good luck," Scout told her.

"Will you help me?" she asked Scout suddenly shy.

Letters from Home 228

"Yeah," he grinned and unhooked it and held the bass by the mouth. Quinn grabbed his cell phone and snapped a photo quickly as she scrunched her nose touching the fish and finding it slimy and told her to smile to get the second picture of them all standing behind her, Scout knelt beside her holding the fish up all of them grinning.

A horn honked, and Evie looked at Scout, "You going to through him back?"

"That's up to you, you don't want to eat him?"

"No," she shook her head. Making another grossed out face. It was such an innocent conversation it helped them to relax more, Scout felt at home instantly, Mercer felt the peacefulness of the area and sighed. He had been there before and felt like it was home. He was happy to have the quiet around Skye and Scout's home for a while so he could get used to the idea of being back in the states, to remember it was safe.

Zane noticed an older woman walking up the hill and Evie smiled, "Gigi look! I got a fish!"

"Wow! Did someone take a picture of that big bass for you?"

"Yeah!" she turned to Quinn, "What was your name again?"

"Quinn," he smiled, "Alright Evie you better tell the fish bye before he's tossed back in."

"Bye Mr. Fish!" she waved as Scout tossed him back into the pond.

"How are you Mrs. Miller?" Scout turned and swiped his hands on his pants before standing.

"I'm good, is Skye not here?" she cocked her head.

"She had a call at two this morning an apartment fire near Oakland Hospital, they were sending their overflow to Elizabethtown, so she was called in," Scout shook his head, "I haven't seen her since then."

"I saw on the news over seven hundred wounded," she sighed, "Well thank you boys for watching Princess Evie. I've heard about a lot of you boys from Serabeth and Shawn."

"It was nice to meet you ma'am, we will see you later then?" Quinn asked aware that Zane was uncharacteristically quiet.

"Yes," she smiled, "Come on Evie we best get lunch ready for Aunt Sera when she gets home."

"Bye!" Evie waved smiling.

"Bye Evie," Scout smiled.

They continued to fish and then went to the house to get lunch before sitting on the porch. Skye pulled in and walked up to the porch finding she had doubled the number of Marines since the time she left. She sat next to Scout and set her head on his shoulder, "So introduce your friends, Scout."

"This is Zane and Quinn," he pointed to each, and she smiled, "Have you went to find Rashel and Zaidee?"

"We met Zaidee when we went for breakfast, Rashel was there with her dad getting coffee," Quinn nodded, "We met Princess Evie and her Gigi."

"Sounds like a busy day," she smiled, "Did you catch any fish?"

"How'd you know we went fishing?" Zane frowned confused. It felt comfortable like a favorite shirt or comfort food; the house, the cousins, everything made it scream home to all of them.

"I know my cousin," she laughed, "If he caught anything we can cook fish for supper."

"Actually, you need to go take a shower and get ready, we are going out," Scout smiled.

"I need some entertainment," she gave a tired smile.

"That bad of a day huh?" he squeezed her shoulders.

"Only highlight was knowing you were home and waiting for me to finish up," she grinned, "How'd you boys sleep anyway?"

Derek met her gaze in surprise, "Good, felt like home. I think it was the best sleep I've had in a long time."

"Good," she smiled, "Alright, give me an hour and I'll be back down."

They were all wearing normal clothes for the first time in what felt like ages. Scout grinned, "I'm counting, Skye."

She went upstairs and raced to get ready, she heard Scout on the phone, "I will let her know, we will be right there."

"What's wrong?" she noticed it was her phone.

"We have a stop to make," he flashed a smile, "You clean up nice without the bedhead, Skye."

"Ha-ha," she rolled her eyes, "Are we riding together? My car has six seats."

"Sure," Scout nodded, "I'm driving."

He knew she was tired, and no amount of makeup would hide the fact from him. He didn't want her to drive that tired. Skye got into the middle in the front seat and Derek took the passenger seat as Quinn and Zane got in the back. "Where are we headed, Scout?" she frowned seeing they were headed toward the edge of town. The library doubled as the local community center and there were tons of cars. She frowned and asked, "Was someone hurt during their party? Why didn't they just stop at the hospital?"

"I don't know," he shrugged pulling in and Derek let her out and they followed behind her. She glanced around to find everyone standing and clapping. Every Marine wore their USMC t-shirt and she glanced around to find Adelina recording, the other girls standing around with their pen pals. She looked back at Scout, "You scared me for no reason!"

"This was for all of us to meet our pen pals," he was suddenly the mature Commander she heard his men talk about.

"We also wanted to thank you for giving us a piece of home when we needed it most," Toby stepped up, "I'm Toby."

"I've heard about you, how's your head?" she shook his hand as he laughed.

"Hard to hurt," he grinned, "Thank you for making this possible and rallying the girls to write to us."

She noticed Martha with the boys sitting with Nadira. They had a huge grill outside the door and two of the Marines were cooking with their families. Beer chilled in a cooler to one side for those that wanted it. She grabbed a water and found Derek standing nearby, "I want you to meet my family, Skye."

"Okay," she nodded surprised as he rubbed his neck. His sister gave her a tight hug and his nephews hugged Derek tight, his parents sat watching quietly knowing they came in just before him and would have a private welcome soon enough. Derek kissed his mom and hugged his dad before sitting with Scout and Skye at the Mercer family table.

"What's this that the guys have to cook their own meal?" she asked Scout and Adelina surprised them with appearing behind Derek's parents.

"I was told they hadn't cooked in a while and they wanted to man the grill because it's a man's job to grill," she rolled her eyes, "I didn't argue with them."

"Uncle Derek when did you get here?"

"Late last night," he smiled, "I couldn't wait for you to finally get here. Did grandpa drive slow enough or was it mom?"

"Mom," they all grinned as their mom rolled her eyes.

"Where's Jim at?" Derek asked his sister and she smiled—her fiancé was polar opposite from her first husband and the entire family loved him, "Couldn't get off work. He can't wait to see you when you get home."

"I can't wait to see him too," Derek smiled realizing he didn't smile often enough lately, it felt foreign to him, and Scout grinned.

"About time you started smiling more," Scout chuckled softly touching his shoulder.

"Commander Chase!" Gryffin held a tray of food putting it on a table, "We are almost ready."

"Alright Gryffin," he nodded and stood gaining everyone's attention. He stepped to the front of the building, "Good evening, everyone!"

Everyone returned the greeting finding seats quickly. Scout looked at Skye, "We are almost ready to enjoy a great meal with great company. It's been a hard tour, but we made it through with a ton of support from our home team here, you guys are awesome!"

The Marines all clapped again, when the whistling died down and it was quiet again, Scout continued, "We want to recognize our pen pals and our video master for encouraging us, for praying continuously when we desperately needed it. If we can circle up as best as possible, I would like to ask Skye to pray over the food. As some of you are aware she's our Platoon prayer warrior and doctor and although we are home, we know she will always be praying for us."

Skye stood and noticed everyone held a hand and it zigzagged through the building and she had Derek's hand and Scout's hand as he moved back to her side. Both warm from the late summer heat, but not uncomfortably hot. She said in a clear voice, "If you all would close your eyes and bow your heads. God thank you for bringing our boys home safe, for blessing us with time together to fellowship and enjoy some relaxation and great smelling food. Bless this food and those that prepared it, for those that eat it and let us have plenty of laughs over it. In Jesus name, and all God's people said?"

Amen rang through the building. She looked to Scout and as everyone sat again, she turned to look at everyone. "You know I was told we were going out to eat and heard Scout on the phone saying there was an emergency. I am thankful to have you here in my hometown to meet all of you and would like to make a small announcement as the guys finish setting the food up...Adelina get your nose out from behind that video camera, so everyone can see you."

Adelina looked up from the screen distracted and looked at everyone in surprise that they were looking back at her, she gave a nervous wave. Skye continued, "A week ago we got exciting news for your video master. She planned to go to college in a year but because most the United States has heard of her video letters; she has received grants and scholarships to go this fall. She is raising money to cover the rest of the expenses and in exchange for this she is heading up the Pen Pal Project at Chattanooga University when she arrives on campus. She and other students will be sending videos to men and women overseas fighting for this nation. If you want to contribute or follow her, please like her Facebook page and I was informed there is a small table in the corner near Serabeth and Princess Evie for you to write your email and other information down and if you want to donate, please do it there. Whatever you need to keep in touch with her. How about a round applause for her hard work as the Video Master!"

They all clapped some men stood; they knew she had worked non-stop to make it happen. Skye sat and found Adelina blushing recording them, Scout looked to Gryffin, "And food is ready!"

His voice boomed everyone slowly made their way to the tables, Skye noticed the red table clothes and welcome home banners. She noticed it was a serve yourself type set up as people went through the line. Scout turned to her, "You are working tomorrow?"

"No," she shook her head, "It's my day off."

"Jack Ewing and his wife are driving all of us to the cemetery tomorrow. I want you to come with me," he met her gaze. The bus drivers in town rarely drove outside of town except for the rare funeral like Johnny's family. She noticed Julie and Jayla coming up to Scout. Jayla hugged him tight, "Thanks for the invite, Scout."

"Adelina set this all up," he shook his head, "They just put my name on it."

"Derek," Julie smiled seeing the young man sitting by his nephews, they had all moved around the table since his sister needed help with the boys.

Letters from Home

"Mrs. Miles," he stood up instantly and came to attention as if on default over the months.

"Oh, just give me a hug," she swiped her eyes reminded of Johnny's time with Derek at the house.

"I-I," he couldn't say the words as the older woman hugged him.

"It's okay," she whispered, "He'd be mad for no pranks tonight, Derek."

"Maybe tomorrow," his voice rough with emotions he tried to fight. She held him tight, her hand smoothing his hair as if he was her own, she was trying to calm down.

"Before you go home, I want you to come by the house alright?" she asked seriously pulling back to see his eyes glassy as he blinked the tears back.

"Yes, ma'am," he nodded.

"Go get food before you blow away," she ordered them all sitting there, "Come on Skye, I haven't seen you eat anything in over a month, you haven't went to CoffeeZ or the restaurant in that long."

"How would you know that?" she asked aware she was right, but Skye wondered how the older woman knew.

"I have eyes and ears everywhere, young lady, come on," she held her hand up and Skye took it following her to the loaded tables. Kids went outside to play on the playground, everyone relaxed sitting at tables. Gryffin came up to Skye and hesitated.

"I've wanted to say hello, but I feel terrible about your sky diving trip," he said shifting his weight from one foot to the other as he studied her.

Letters from Home

"I don't hold it against you, Gryffin," she smiled, "I would go on a hike with you, but I won't jump out of a perfectly good airplane…ever again!"

He chuckled and shook her hand, "Thanks for pulling the girls together to write to us, we needed it. Maybe you can show us some trails to hike around here."

"Definitely," Kevin agreed coming up, agreeing to both the writing and hiking. Laikynn smiled as he spoke up, "You don't realize how bad you need something until you get it. It was a breath of fresh air to get mail and reminded of home. Even if Laikynn intimidates me sometimes."

"What?" she cried sitting next to Kevin's wife, "How?"

"She's super smart," Kevin told Skye, "Sometimes I had Frank who is like a human dictionary on the team read my letters to make sure they were spelled right and didn't sound stupid."

Skye laughed, "Laikynn wouldn't care if there were misspelled words, Kevin."

He went to sit down with Gryffin and Alara nearby. Skye turned to Scout, "He's so quiet and stayed away out of the video of the party."

"People think he's uncomfortable and don't realize that what they take for quiet and uncomfortable is a human tank," Derek said across the table, "He's a lot smarter than he gives himself credit for."

Zane had met Sera and saw the sudden uncertainty in her eyes when he introduced himself and gave her the letter from Shawn so long ago. They had ended up at a table together, Sera had sat with him, his family, and Brian's family. They didn't talk until after the meal, not wanting to ruin it for Evie or the others at their table.

She met his gaze as Evie slept on her lap, Zane had known Sera would worry if he wanted to take Evie away considering he had contacted a lawyer as soon as he heard about Shawn to find out if she was taken care of and if it was possible to move her to his hometown where he lived near his parents.

"Sera," he sat next to her and her mother after throwing away the trash, "I plan to move closer to town and I want to be a part of Evie's life. I don't want her to be uprooted from family, the lawyer I sent was just to make sure she was with family and that she was cared for, I would have moved her to my hometown if she didn't have the care she needed. I know we don't know each other well but I would never tear a little girl from her family. Shawn would kill me if I did that to you guys."

"Shawn never told me about having a godfather for Evie, only that I was the godmother. When the lawyer came, I was worried we would have a custody battle and Evie would be put in the middle after everything she'd already been through. I heard of you but didn't put two and two together since the lawyer said Mr. Wolf and we pen pals call you Zane."

Zane met her gaze and looked down at Evie who was sleeping in her lap, "Shawn was a brother to me, one I never had before. I want to do as much as I can for Evie without being overbearing to you and Mrs. Miller. I know you don't know me well, but I want to do my part, what Shawn wanted. Martha will be looking for me a place close by and I plan to visit once I settle things and see family.

"Breakfast at CoffeeZ in the morning?" Sera offered an olive branch and he agreed.

The party ended late, everyone went to the hotel that came from out of town, all party goers wanting sleep. Marjorie promised to take care of them. Skye sat in the middle again and started to fall asleep as they drove back home.

Zane had been quiet in the backseat as they drove to Skye's house, it had went well and all the Marines planned to stay in town for a few days to rest before going home. He was going to meet Sera for breakfast and after they came back from the cemetery, they would meet Shawn's family. Quinn was quiet having heard the conversation and knowing Skye was asleep in the front seat they all were quiet. Scout packed Skye to her room and laid her down. She woke for a moment, "Make sure Derek is comfortable for me, Scout."

"I will," he smiled, leave it to her to think of others first. He turned to find the guys watching from the door. They went to the front porch and listened to the crickets for a long time, "You going to the hotel to be closer to your families?"

"Zane and I are," Quinn nodded.

"Adelina made the comment that the hotel is full of everyone staying so if it's alright I will stay here until things calm down," Derek murmured.

"Any time," Scout nodded, "You boys know you are always welcome we just don't have enough rooms for everyone at once."

"Yes, sir," they murmured, and Zane and Quinn left shortly after.

The next day they all got on buses, Adelina rode along sitting in the silent bus. All the men were dressed in their class A uniform and when they pulled into the cemetery, they all went to Johnny's where everyone stood in silent. Skye stood next to Scout and each man took a moment, most had coins they set on the stone. Scout was last, following Derek whose shoulders had shook as he stood over his friend's grave. Skye let Scout

Letters from Home 239

step forward, but he caught her hand, he wanted her with him. The coins were set with care, overlaying each other, and shining in the sunlight. Scout sighed, "I'll miss you, Johnny."

He set the last coin on the stone and saluted, Skye didn't notice the other men had formed ranks and saluted as well. Only Adelina caught the moment on video from the bus. She stood near Shawn Miller's grave and when they headed back to the bus, she went up to pay her respects and recorded the name with all the coins, "Loved, missed, but never forgotten."

The guys stopped at Shawn's grave to pay respect to the others that they had lost. Shawn had been the first one in Scout's platoon to be lost on their second tour, most the platoon knew him except the newer members who were quiet in the back watching. They loaded the buses, some family members came, the Miles family declined the invite—wanting the boys to have a moment to mourn but telling them that they would meet them for supper that night at the restaurant in town.

They went home in silence, the bus was bumpy, but no one made a sound. Skye sat with Scout toward the front of the bus, Kane and Derek sat next to them. Skye sat in the aisle and touched Derek's hand seeing his tears streak down his face but made no move to comment. She had brought boxes of tissues and had them sitting every few seats back on each bus. Derek accepted the tissues in his free hand and didn't care that she held his hand in front of the others. The phone calls and letters made him feel close to her. They mainly talked about Johnny for the first few phone calls, slowly he started diving into her life, she asked questions too but not many because she didn't want to be pushy. Her hand over his, Derek studied it, focused on it so he could get his emotions back in the tightly sealed box he tried to keep them in.

The week went by, and families took their Marine home until Derek was the only one left, his parents and sister had already left but he sat on Skye's porch in silence as she walked up in scrubs. She sat next to him on the swing and studied the fields and listened to the wind blowing through the trees and the birds singing.

"I'm dreading the city," he admitted.

"You always have a place to stay if it gets to be too much," she shrugged, "I dread the city every time I have to drive through it, I couldn't imagine living in it."

Her amused tone made him look over at her, "Scout said you want the living room rewired, he plans to do that next week sometime. You mind if he has help?"

"Not at all," she shook her head.

"Thanks for everything Skye," he murmured, "You don't know what it means."

"No, I don't but I'm glad I could help, Derek."

"The bible in the room, is that one of your first bibles?"

"Yeah," she cocked her head and pushed her hair out of her face, "Why?"

"I've been reading it," he murmured, "It helps."

"You can keep it if you need it," she offered, "It was there for a reason."

"How do you stay positive and say the things I always need to hear?" his brow knit, and he searched her eyes, seeing that now there weren't tired rings under them and they were bright—as if having them there made her happy.

"Pray, read the bible, have faith that God won't let me fall on my face," she chuckled.

"I'll leave it in case someone else needs it too and for when I visit. I got a bible collecting dust at home."

"Okay, did you tell Scout?"

"He said he figured I'd be back to help him, called you a slave driver giving him that to-do list so soon."

Skye frowned as Derek smirked, a dimple appearing as he relaxed against the swing. Skye sighed, "I know how he gets if he can't find something to keep his hands busy."

Derek stood and slung a small backpack over his shoulder. His sister had taken a majority of his stuff home and brought his motorcycle on a trailer behind her SUV. He swung onto it as Scout came around the house, "See you soon, Derek!"

"Yes, sir," he said over the roar of the engine, and he took off. Scout looked at Skye to see her eyes tracking him down the driveway.

"You good, Skye?"

"Yes…yeah," she nodded the emotions she was experiencing were confusing, she barely knew Derek, yet she was disappointed to see him go, "I hope he's alright in the city. You all have been through a lot this last tour."

"He knows he has a safe place to come," Scout murmured taking Derek's seat, "Kane has Sera's younger brother helping him design a house for a class project."

"Good," Skye murmured and sighed, "You want to go get coffee at Zaidee's?"

"Sure," he smiled knowing she had another late night. She wasn't nearly as tired as she was when they first got home, less stress about the Marines showed in her eyes and her bounce in each step when she walked showed her happiness.

Letters from Home

She was heading in to change when she turned back to look at him.

"Hey, I had a question, I noticed a large shoebox under your bed, are those shoes you can't fit in your closet?" Scout had a feeling they weren't, but he wanted to know without snooping.

"No," she shook her head, "I'll show you."

She went to her room and pulled out the shoebox. She went downstairs and opened it. He frowned at all the envelopes. There was a cardboard divider in the middle, and he took the first to the right. The address was Kandahar Afghanistan, his name on the top, it was his first tour overseas, the first letter he wrote to her. How did he miss she kept his letters under her bed?

She pulled the other side to show the same address with J. Miles on the top, "I keep every letter I get from you all. I have Johnny's, yours, and a few others who wrote me while they were on tours. The others are in a different shoebox."

"You want to see something?" he asked standing up and going to his room. She sat closing the shoebox and setting it beside her. Scout came out and showed her a plastic tote he kept in his room. He opened it to show all her letters. "Johnny has one similar in his room as well from the other tours."

"His mom gave me the letters from this tour," she nodded lightly, "I don't know that she's went through his room, but she wanted me to have my letters."

Scout pulled the first letter out, it was a favorite of his, "Scout if you hadn't written me your address, I would have left these letters in your room for when you came home. I would've been royal ticked off!"

"Oh geez," she giggled, and he folded it carefully putting it away.

Letters from Home

"Let's go get coffee," he murmured.

"Okay," she nodded, they put their letters safely away, Skye changed clothes, and went to CoffeeZ. They sat and relaxed as the entire room slowly emptied and only one man came up to them. He was a retired Marine who served in Vietnam, "Welcome home, Scout."

"Thank you, sir," Scout nodded, "It's good to be home."

That evening when Skye grabbed her Bible, she found an envelope in Psalms and she frowned confused at it, her name was in cursive across the front.

Dear Skye,

You don't know how much I needed your letters. I don't know that I could have survived without your encouragement. I know it doesn't make sense that I never wrote you. I didn't want to corrupt you, I still don't, and by corrupt, I mean make you see the world through my eyes, full of negativity and such. Thank you for continuing to write to me, I know it was probably harder than I can imagine, and I couldn't possibly make it up to you. Even writing this, having talked, and gotten to know you, is harder than I thought it would be. You deserve the world, Skye; you helped us all through Hell and out the other side.

See you soon,

Derek Mercer

Epilogue
Three years later

Adelina came home as a college graduate, during her summers she traveled and made videos, each semester every student picked a military man or woman and did a long video for each of them as their senior project. Adelina was still in her element and traveled all the time to work with different nonprofits who requested some help. She tried to make it to every single one or send someone to go.

Lance Eldridge continued to teach at Chattanooga and support the students to serve their country with nonprofits as well as working a normal job. He became head over the film department, and it became the new Chattanooga University culture to work with nonprofits and doing a small film scholarship to a winner who made the best. The judges were major producers who welcomed the change wholeheartedly.

Most the pen pals from three years ago served stateside and many moved closer to Elizabethtown having created lifelong friends through ink on a page. Kevin retired from the Marines and had four children, every vacation was made to see Laikynn and visit Scout. Gryffin took Alara on a mountain climbing trip in which she loved, and they planned a rock-climbing trip each year. Zane moved to Elizabethtown and helped to raise Evie, Scout had a bet with Derek that Sera and Zane would be married in another year or two.

Derek Mercer moved to Elizabethtown, not able to stay in the big city he bought a couple acres next to Rashel, and married Skyelar who became Doctor Skyelar Mercer and had two little boys of their own, the oldest named Johnny in memory of their best friend. Kane and Martha were their neighbors, and their children grew up as thick as thieves.

Letters from Home

Quinn and Brian lived a town over having started their own families and worked closely with Serabeth's younger brother in the construction industry. Once a year everyone got together deep in the woods, the same place the Miles' family camped, and enjoyed hearing of what happened in the last year. Quinn's dog Dude never quit barking, but they didn't mind.

Scout lived in the farmhouse and was dating Laikynn and farming the land. He told Skye that they served their country and he retired. Skye and Dr. Walsh were the two VA doctors in town for the veterans converging on the small town. Laikynn thought it funny that now each house of the retired Marines had guest rooms set like Skye's farmhouse. A bible under the bedside table and home to anyone that needed it.

Derek had told Skye he wanted the bible and showed her the letter Johnny had left for anyone that found it, she was surprised Johnny had done something like that. He didn't bring up faith often only ever told Skye he knew where he was headed, and she had nothing to worry about. Derek and Scout opened a nonprofit for military suffering PTSD to come hang out and recover in the quiet of a small town. Kane and the others volunteered all the time and they stayed pretty busy. Adelina came home often to make videos and advertise for them. Still calling her videos for the guys Letters from Home, they told her the name was Transitioning Home. The next step to coming home, dealing with the culture shock, and preparing to go home. Adelina was preparing to go overseas to get a glimpse of what it was like, working hand in hand with the Marines from basics to transitioning home and retiring and she loved it. She was the leader in military videos and news, Lettie Joseph was in front of Adelina's camera more times than either could count, working to educate the population on the life of their military men and women.

The End

Made in the USA
Columbia, SC
07 September 2023

b4b165d3-3d70-4f19-819a-dbded9eed6caR01